Undertow

SHORT STORIES
by Virginia Dansereau

KALAMALKA PRESS

Feb 25/08
For Barb. Thank you
for sharing my "special"
evening.
Love,
Virginia

Cover design by Christine McPhee and Kalamalka Press.
© Kalamalka Press, Virginia Dansereau

Published in 2008 by the Kalamalka Press
An imprint of the Kalamalka Institute for Working Writers
of Okanagan College, 7000 College Way, Vernon, BC, V1B
2N5, Canada

The Kalamalka Press Board of Directors is John Lent,
Craig McLuckie, Ross Tyner, Francie Greenslade and
James Hamilton.

This volume was edited by John Lent.

Library and Archives Canada Cataloguing in Publication

Dansereau, Virginia,

      Undertow: short fiction / Virginia Dansereau.

ISBN   978-0-9738057-5-8

Cover Illustration: Christine McPhee and Kalamalka Press.

Printed in Canada by Okanagan College Print Services,
Kelowna.

Dedications

*For my mother, Natalie Fassett, who taught me to read, and
raised, cleaned and sold chickens door to door
to send me to high school.
For my uncle, Michael Ukas, who helped finance my education,
sent our family boxes of books, and wrote me letters
of encouragement when I was a child.*

Also

*In memory of my husband, Georges Dansereau,
who watched me scribble endlessly
without asking what on earth I was doing,
and Dennis Dansereau,
who was gifted with creativity
but lost his way.*

Acknowledgements:

'Undertow' and 'The Chair' won 1st and 3rd prizes consecutively in the 2000 Okanagan University College Short Story Contest. They were published in Chapbook form by RSVP (Really Small Vernon Press) of Vernon, BC. 'The Harrow Man' won Honourable Mention in the 2001 Canadian Authors Association Short Story Contest. It was published in *Winners' Circle 10* in 2003. 'White Daisies' appeared in *Who Lies Beautifully: The Kalamalka Anthology* (2002), Kalamalka Press, and 'Shallow Water' appeared in *Other Voices* (1991) and the *Fat Moon* anthology (1993). 'Sky City' was a runner-up in the 2002 New Writers Prize in England and short-listed for the 2003 Okanagan University College Short Story Contest.

A hearty thank you to my creative writing instructors: John Lent, Lorna Crozier, Patrick Lane, Sandy Duncan and Edna Alford. They taught me to pursue my own voice and to use my imagination. As well, their encouragement kept me on a path that was often riddled with obstacles.

Also, a grateful thank you to my patient and highly skilled editors, John Lent and Edna Alford; and the following people who have read some of the stories and given me critical feed-back: Glen Sorestad, Suzan Milburn, Norman Slingsby, Tish Woodley, and Al Scott.

In addition, I wish to express appreciation to the Banff School of Fine Arts Writing Studio, the Sage Hill Writing Experience and a Cypress Hills workshop where I've been able to hone my skills unemcumbered by the hectic nature of everyday living.

Contents:

UNDERTOW

I'm broken and I can't be fixed. My hairy-chested, holier than thou Anton has tried to fix me. My hand-wringing mother. A shrink they hired as a last resort. But, I'm not fixable. There are no spare parts to be bought. Not new. Not old. Mind you, there was one fixable part - my tubes. But I guess they don't really count, being body parts. I got them tied up. No more eggs for fertilization. No more eggs to grow a howling bundle of arms and legs I have no idea how to look after. The books say women have maternal instincts that kick in when needed. Mine are dead.

I shake babies when they cry. Ask the guy in the truck who watched me and later reported me. "It wasn't the shaking that bothered me so much," the man told Social Services, "but the clenched teeth while she was doing it."

*

I sit on the deck of a Costa Rican cottage, cicadas singing, a hawk calling, the bamboo creaking. I sit here pen in hand, a glass of freshly squeezed orange juice on the table beside me. Mario, my landlord, brings me juice every morning. An envelope addressed to Anton and my son lies beside the glass, but the paper in my lap remains blank. I'm not sure yet if I want them to find me.

There's a mandarin orange tree just outside my door. I can walk out anytime, circle an orange with my fingers, feel its weight in my palm, and pull. The peelings fall into my hands without my being conscious of them. I know I've just eaten another orange when I smell my fingers. They smell bitter and sweet.

It's nice here. I walk through coffee plantations, look across the hills and valleys, and watch bananas grow out of huge purple flowers shaped like tear drops. San Jose is down below: its bustle of people and cars; its airport. There's a ticket in my duffle bag. I have two months left before I must return to Canada. To see my son. See Anton.

Anton won't want me anymore, though. Not after the search I've put him through.

Anton thinks one's basic organs have been given for a reason; that they shouldn't be tampered with. I think I was given mine to tempt the devil.

I'm quite evil. I accept that now. But sh-h-h. I don't want to talk about it.

*

I swim in the pool here. Under and up. Under and up. Anton liked to swim in the ocean. Sometimes, I wished he'd stay under. When Anton swam, I walked the shore and searched for shells. They're beautiful in this country, large knobby half shells, smooth tear-drops. I collected the delicate ones when I was still with Anton. The kind that would crush beneath your thumb if pressed even slightly.

Mario's Rottweiler, Pico, comes to visit. She's heavy with pups and walks laboriously. Perhaps she has more pups than usual tucked up in the horns of her uterus. Like overgrown beans in lima pods. She eases her swollen body down beneath my hammock. The hammock's sway seems to comfort her. She's weary, but always wary. Keeps her ears cocked for unusual sounds.

Pico and I sit together for hours at a time. I do nothing while we sit. Just look straight ahead. Listen for toucans. I'm never sure if I hear real toucans or the landlord's wife. She can imitate them perfectly. I'm glad I'm here in Toucan country instead of howler monkey territory. Howlers scare the bee-Jesus out of me. They sound as if they've been badly hurt and make me think I did something to cause their pain.

I'm in this cottage because of the turtles. The ones Anton and I got up in the middle of the night to go see. How strange that night was: the sky black, the echo of someone calling "Turtles, turtles," from his truck and the bumpy ride to a river crossing. Anton wouldn't hold my hand on the rowboat. Wouldn't even walk beside me on the dark expanse of sand. He was still angry from the afternoon when I'd said, "No sex. I don't know if the ligation has taken."

"It's called making love, Rhea," he'd said. "I just want to make love to you."

"It's sex," I said. "As long as there's a chance of making babies, it's sex."

"Is that so bad?" he asked. I don't know why he needed to ask. He's delusional, I guess. That's a great word, delusional. Shrinks use words like that. It makes them sound smarter than you.

I walked alone on that dark beach, falling far behind the tour group. The ocean slapped the shore and the breeze ruffled my hair. Ahead, the moustached guide shined a flashlight covered with something red so as not to alarm the turtles. We walked a long time under the Milky Way. Signs warned of high tides. I tried to figure out how a turtle would handle a high tide. Or the pull of undertow. What if she ended up on the wrong beach?

As I approached the others, I heard the guide say, "There." He pointed to a shape heaving itself out of the water several yards up the beach. We waited and watched as the leatherback climbed up the bank and dug a hole. Sand flew in all directions. We then tiptoed up the bank and quietly circled her. She was gargantuan, weighing more than three hundred pounds. Eggs dropped from her tilted body into the hole beneath her.

"She'll lay over one hundred," the guide whispered.

The eggs lying there like that looked so vulnerable I wanted to take off my clothes and cover them. Anton watched, mesmerized, the way he watched me when I gave birth to my son. I sighed with relief when the turtle began flicking her back flippers to cover the eggs with sand. I backed away to avoid the sting of sand on my bare feet.

"Even though the turtle leaves no trace of being here," the guide whispered again, "only one of the turtles hatched will make it to water."

I looked at Anton's rigid back and suddenly got a flash of the guide's truck keys dangling from the ignition. He'd parked the truck under a tree across the river. I felt curiously settled even though my next move was to wander into the dark alone.

*

Pico stands up and sniffs the cuffs of my sweater. Perhaps she favours it for the whelping box that Mario and I prepared for her.

"No you don't, Pico," I tell her, shaking her muzzle in my hands. "I can't part with my sweater." I had only bought one of each thing in the market located beside the place I dumped the truck. I need the sweater because it's cool at night and I don't sleep.

Although the clothes were local, I didn't look local. So I bought brown hair dye and applied it thickly over my red hair. Now that I'm tanned and my freckles resemble skin blemishes, I look like a shadow of my fairer self.

To stay undetected, I got off the bus routes and found this cottage. No one had rented it because of the dog. I'm used to guard dogs. I helped my father raise and train Doberman Pinchers. He said I was a natural, that I understood their basic instincts.

Maybe that was a compliment. Maybe he didn't expect me to be good all the time, just manageable. I should have married someone like him. Good triumphing over evil might not have been so important. I'm not blaming Anton for my weaknesses, just for his blindness. "Sh-h-h," he'd always say when I tried to tell him something negative, "think good thoughts." Anton had asked me to attend church services with him, but I've never been comfortable in one room buildings. There's nowhere to hide. Besides, I'm not good enough for God.

I wish I had let Anton take my son to the services, though. He's good enough. He has warm, friendly arms that are solid and roomy. Mine are spindly and clumsy.

My mother has him, my son. It's her part in the scheme to get my mind into a different space and maybe go back cured. The counselor gave up on me. He said, "I can't help you, Rhea, if you don't talk to me." I just sat in his office week after week and grinned. It humoured me how Anton could tell me not to think dark thoughts or to talk about them, then pay seventy dollars an hour to make me do it.

My mother kept wringing her hands. She was afraid it was something she'd done. Ha! Evil can go back generations. Maybe I'm like my great, great, great Aunt Dora whom my family hushed up about whenever someone pointed her out in a photograph album.

Maybe she haunts my soul. Anton would have to hire an exorcist in that case.

*

A Japanese screen divides the kitchen from the bedroom in my cottage. Windows open out to the bamboo trees and the flowering Ylang Ylang. The flower's fragrance wafts in. It's as sweet as the taste of nectar in nasturtiums.

I sauté the chicken the yardman gave me and watch Pico's nose crinkle up in anticipation. When the meat's cooked, I throw her several portions. It's one of the perks of her pregnancy. She gulps down each piece hardly tasting it. Perhaps smell is more important than taste for dogs. I think of my pregnancy and the three, four and five oranges I'd eat in one sitting. I ate them slowly, though, relishing each succulent portion.

Pico moans and begins to pace back and forth. "Time for your box," I tell her, locating a flashlight to lead her back to the main house. She climbs into the whelping box and settles down, a look of relief in her watery brown eyes. I check the supplies. Mario fetches a pail of warm water, fingers the wash cloths and soap, shakes the iodine and fills a hot water bottle. Then, he sits down beside me for the watch.

When Pico expels the first pup, she begins to clean it up, but must leave it because the next one's head is surfacing. I pick up the pup, remove the membrane and hold its head down to drain all the fluid from its lungs. Mario reaches for the wet and shaking pup and wraps it in a towel to dry. He places it on the hot water bottle. He is so gentle. I imagine his hands soft as his voice. His voice is like rain on a still evening. I look at my hands and feel awkward. My fingers seem like claws. I see a cigarette clutched in them. It's hanging dangerously close to a baby's bare skin.

I back away from the whelping box, plunge the wash cloths into the pail of water and shove some dry towels into Mario's hands. As I watch Mario wrap each puppy in a towel and hold it close to his chest, I see Anton's arms reach out to take my son from me. My son is crying. Anton envelops him in his arms and holds him gently, but firmly. He caresses my son's face with the soft pads of his fingers. My son whimpers, then gurgles and slips off to sleep.

"He'll be fine with Anton," I hear myself saying. Mario looks up at me, his face a question mark. "They'll be fine, Mario," I say, and then turn to leave.

*

I rock in my hammock, trying to match the creaks of the rope with that of the bamboo. It's pitch dark, but I don't use lights. Shadows frighten me more than the dark. I rock back and forth, back and forth. Creak. Creak. I feel as stiff as the bamboo stalks rubbing against one another. Something falls inside the bamboo. It sounds like rain. Similarly, tears run down my cheeks unchecked. I only know they're falling when I touch my shirt and feel the dampness.

Maybe I did love my baby. Do love him.

I drift off to sleep wondering who will teach my son to cry now that I'm not there. And I dream my arms and hands are as gentle as Mario's. They detach from my body and float about looking for my baby. They find him in his cradle and reach out for him, but just before he succumbs to them he sees my face. He bares his teeth and snarls. I wake in a cold sweat.

*

All of the pups but the first-born are thriving. Pico carries it over to my porch several times a day. It's the only one she allows me to touch. I place the pup on my sweater in my lap. She snuggles into it then lifts her head to accept the milk I drop from an eye dropper. I rock the pup and watch a chameleon climb the wall. For a moment, I think it possible to change. I actually feel like something in me is changing. That black may turn into pale grey, at least. Perhaps it's the sun doing it. The warm air. The cottage all to myself. Pico and her pups.

Now that Mario and I have pups to talk about, he often comes over and sits on my deck. The day the pups turn six weeks old, he says, "Rhea, why don't you stay and train the pups?"

I look away, study the stand of bamboo, how each section appears screwed together. How the green stripes look like tears running down the stalks.

"I've watched you with Pico," he says. "You can do it." He seems to realize I need that reassurance. He tells me a guard dog beats placing broken glass on rooftops and concrete fences. "Trained dogs bring in a good price," he says. "In exchange, you can have the cottage rent-free and I'll get the yardman to clear some garden space for you."

If I take Mario up on his offer, I may be a fugitive for the rest of my life. I think Mario knows this. Maybe he saw my picture in the paper. Or maybe someone mentioned my name. I didn't change my first name. It means mother.

WHITE DAISIES

I didn't want Fern to look like just any scarecrow. "No stitched eyes and crooked nose for you," I said, when I bought her head. "And, definitely no straw." I stuffed her body with Fiberfil. And, when we shopped, I told her to keep her eyes open for something unique; something that would set her apart from every other scarecrow.

It was difficult for her at first; she was naturally drawn to the department store tables of straw hats and plaid shirts. "No, Fern," I said, "let's look at scarves. A bright polyester scarf to wind around your head and knot at the side." Once the idea took hold, she rushed ahead of me into boutiques and began modelling had designed silk. Much as I hated to, I had to be practical and insist on polyester. "Silk will never stand up to the elements," I explained. "It'll wrinkle and shrivel and you'll look like a beat up old thing in no time at all."

We bought a blue scarf with wild white daisies on it. I don't know why I insisted on this one when she liked wild roses. After the scarf, there was no looking back. Fern insisted on things I hadn't even thought of, like a rope belt decorated with big brass coins and brown leather sandals laced up with several strands of black ankle ribbons. I added the basics - a long, beige skirt, gathered at the waist and flouncy on the bottom, and a blue floral blouse with a collar so large it covered her shoulders and fell half-way down her back.

When I put her up on the post above the grape vines, she looked downright Bohemian. And the smile I painted on her face seemed almost real.

I wish that I could paint a smile on my face. It's been a long time since I've felt like smiling. Three months to be exact. The entire length of time my mother's been with us, wheeling her chair all over the house and bumping into things.

I can stand the nicks in the furniture, but her concern with getting in the way drives me crazy. Even my neighbour commented on it last week. "Why, your mother looks like she'd shrink into a corner if she could," she said. And she would. Even before the stroke, when she could still speak, she never stopped telling me, "I don't want to be any bother, dear, so just tell me what to do in the kitchen and, if I can, I'll do it."

The experts say that small habits developed when young become more pronounced when old. They're right. Mother's pattern of keeping to herself began when I was a child. "To give you and your father quality time together," she'd say. That was on the good days. On bad days, she'd mumble that she didn't want to be a bother and would close the door to her bedroom.

I like to think of her in the earlier years when she directed a crew of harvesters wearing her denim overalls and black rubber boots. I can still see her guiding a grain auger into the granary and hear her laugh with delight when the first kernels bounced off the bottom of the granary. I wish I had more memories like that. Everything else seems to have taken place in the kitchen. "Phyllis, line up everything you need before you start," I hear her saying, her voice dull and flat. "And wash it all up as you use it." Invariably, she'd be looking out of the kitchen window or staring at the blue porcelain mask hanging on the upper cupboard.

There seemed to be a dividing line; pre-kitchen era and kitchen era. My father, too, seemed to draw a dividing line. He stayed outdoors in the summer and the basement in the winter, only coming into the house or upstairs to eat and sleep. Prior to that, he used to help mother with the cooking, singing songs like "Down by the Riverside" and "A Bicycle Built for Two."

For me, kitchen work is totally mundane. I'd rather be out pruning the grapes than lining up flour, baking powder, salt, and milk. The only thing I enjoy doing in the way of measuring ingredients is making wine. I love the whole process from buying and planting the seedlings to bottling the wine. Nothing compares to holding luscious purple clusters of grapes in your hands, then releasing them to their destiny. I even love the wait for ester-formation and the six months in cold storage. It heightens the anticipation of that first sip. That first sip is worth waiting a lifetime for.

My grapes are very important to me. That's why I put Fern in the vineyard. I don't know if she'll really frighten the birds, but she can report every little change and observe the grapes so closely that she might hear them talk to one another. I think grapes talk, don't you? *Good morning. Did you sleep well last night? Yes, the dew was just right. Isn't this a glorious day? I'm sure I'll turn a little purple today. How do you feel?* What I like is the love-talk in early spring when the flowers are just opening and the bees are penetrating each pistil. It's incredibly sexy.

Sexy isn't exactly what you'd call me since Mother arrived. Kent has moved into the spare bedroom because he says looking and not touching is torture. We had a terrible row the day he moved. "Does this mean every time some little thing goes wrong, you're going to move out on me?" I shouted.

"Phyllis," he began, in that soft reasoning tone I hate when angry, "this isn't some little thing. You shrink away from me as if I'm some kind of monster." His eyes narrowed and the ruddiness of his skin deepened.

"You're exaggerating," I said, plunking myself on his bed. "You know I don't mean it. It's just that Mother has always made me self-conscious with you."

"Yeah! Well, maybe it's time you decide who you live with," he said. That sounded like an ultimatum to me, so I stalked off and joined Fern in the vineyard.

"I want to have more control over my life," I told Fern. "I thought buying you and the new clothes would give it to me. I thought your freedom to talk to the wind and the plants and to feel the breeze on the back of your neck would rub off on me." She just looked off into the distance as her skirt whipped around her legs. "All you seem to have done so far is attract Kent." An edge had come into my voice. "Oh, I saw him looking at you this morning. He even turned back after he'd walked half-way to the house."

Mother never came between us in the early years. We lived in a flat in Yorkville, our furniture a mattress and heaps of orange and purple pillows. She hated it. Hated Yorkville. She never forgave herself for talking my father into giving me a trip to Toronto for graduation.

Fortunately, Kent wasn't the reason I stayed, so she liked him. She still likes him, plays endless hours of cards with him. Kent came along months after I took a job in an import shop. He walked right into my life looking so comfortable in his skin that I couldn't resist him. I met him in the shop when he came in to buy a lamp. By the time I'd shown him our supply, he'd found out where each one came from, where I came from and my love for wine-making.

"How on earth did a prairie gopher learn to make wine?" he asked.

"Just like that - being a go-for for my father. He was a wheat farmer, so he didn't have much to do in the winter. To fill in time, he began experimenting with the extra potatoes we grew. Because I was continually escaping from kitchen work and he seemed to have more time for me than my mother, I just naturally fell into helping him."

"Incredible," he said, shaking his head. "Would you believe that I'm studying the fruit growing industry? We'd make a hell of a business team."

We made an even better team than either of us could see. Here we are married, nineteen years later, and running the best grape vineyard and apple orchard for miles around.

It wasn't until we bought this orchard in Naramata that Mother took a fancy to visiting us, two, three, four times a year for two or three weeks at a time. Kent didn't move out on me then. I guess this arrangement looks a little more permanent. Circumstances like this wouldn't make Fern frigid. She'd tease the pants off any guy with that smile and swing of her skirt.

Oh dear, Mother has gone and tipped something over again. It used to be that I was the one knocking things down. I don't think she ever forgave me for bouncing a basketball in the kitchen when I was a child and hitting her precious mask with it. She stood over the smashed item as if I'd killed something, then snatched up two of the pieces and placed them in a little box. Honest to God, you'd have thought the box was a coffin. One of the pieces had a teardrop coursing down its cheek, the other a wide smile. Later, when I found her crying in her bedroom, her face looked just like the mask, big tears rolling down round cheeks and catching in a red, upturned mouth. I remember being so confused.

Mother knocked over my Opium perfume. The lid flew off and the liquid seeped into the rug. I'm afraid my lid flew off too. I screamed at her, something I've worked hard not to do. She's beside herself, banging her left hand on the arm of her chair. She has twisted around so much I have to straighten her and arrange the fabric of her powder blue robe over her legs. Her legs are so thin now, they feel like sticks. Some of the perfume has spilled on her robe, but I need Kent to help me change her. I pat her finally and say, "Never mind, Mother. A rug shampooer will suck it right out."

I'll have to do it quickly, though. It's a good thing I heard her or it might stay in there all day and spread like the milk I spilled when I was ten years old. I scrubbed it and scrubbed it but some of it spread into the underlay. Within a few days, Mother began sniffing around the house and within a week we were pulling up the carpet. I got away with not telling her I did it because I had two friends over when it happened. And now, I yell at her. I'll bet she'd give anything to have a couple of friends around.

"Fern," I say, when I go outside to escape the smell, "what is wrong with me?" Her dark hair separates a little in the breeze and stands in tufts, like a cat's fur does when it's sitting in a tree. The collar on her blouse lifts as if it were slightly inflated. I stare into her olive green eyes and realize the colour and the line along the top of her eyelashes look like Mother's used to. "Blue eyes with navy blue eyeliner are what we want," I say. I run back to the house for the paint. When I bought the head, I was so intent on it having black hair I ignored the eye-colour.

My eyes are blue and my hair used to be black. Black and shiny like a raven's feathers. It's greying now, along the sides and in my bangs. I wore it long until a couple years ago. When I cut it, people said it brought out my face. I wasn't sure I wanted my face to stick out that much, but Mother kept hinting it looked nicer long, so I haven't grown it back out.

Mother's hair is long. When she was young, it was dark brown and thick and wavy. She used to tie it back with ribbons instead of in the French twists all the other mothers wore.

Fern's hair is in a shoulder-length bob. Her face is small too, but she wouldn't let me cut her hair after we bought the scarf. I don't know why I took out the scissors.

There's a faraway look in Fern's eyes, now that they're sky blue. It's as though she wants me to look beyond her, beyond the vineyard. It's so compelling that I walk over to the nearest hill and look down at Okanagan Lake. It possesses an aquamarine hue with streaks of purple where the currents change. I notice the mountain reflections moving in harmony with the waves, elongating into narrow crystal-topped spires, then compressing to low castle-like structures. But, I know that's not what Fern wants me to look at, so I give in to her and raise my eyes to the valley and the clefts of open space between the mountains. The openness takes me back to the prairie setting I grew up in. I'm six years old, and I'm walking through the fields of summer fallow on my father's farm. My step is light. The breeze stirs my hair and my skirt. The wheat ahead of me bends its full heads south-easterly. There are light clouds in the sky, quietly crossing the sun's path and new robins fly about, dipping their wings awkwardly. I hear a laugh. It rises from the wheat like bubbles from the wire hoop I always carry. There are two laughs, my mother's and a man's. It's not my father's laugh.

There's a free and easy sound to the laughter. I see a flash of blue cloth embossed with white daisies as my mother dashes up the dirt road. Her dark, wavy hair flows wild behind her. She disappears behind the shelter of elm trees which surround the house. The man stands up and begins walking toward the railway crossing. He's the Italian farmhand from the adjoining farm. We'd had him at our dinner table many times trying to teach him English.

As I walk back to the house to spell Kent off from watching Mother, I wonder what made me prefer my father's company to Mother's. Neither of them smiled or laughed much.

"I'm back," I call, closing the door quietly so as not to startle Mother.

Kent looks at me accusingly, and asks, "What happened before you left?"

"Nothing," I say. "She just spilled my perfume. I told you about that." Mother's in her chair as usual, but Kent has had to grab the white curtain sash from the living room window to wind around her waist and tie behind the chair.

"She tried to get out of the chair in our room," he explains. "She was looking for something, Phyllis. Stuff is turned upside down all over the room. I tied her into the chair to calm her down. She was thrashing around so much, I thought she'd hurt herself." I can see he's upset. His eyebrows are almost a straight line of red bristles.

I grab a hairbrush and gently brush Mother's hair. With all the excitement, it has come loose from the knot I twisted it into this morning and hangs in wisps. Brushing her hair is the one thing that quiets her. If I take the time to fluff it out on the sides, the stiffness on the right side of her face softens. As I brush, I try to figure out what she wants. She just shakes her head, more like a nod, and silently cries, tears rolling straight down the paralyzed side of her face, and zigzagging along her crooked perpetual half smile on the left.

She begins to shiver, so I fetch her white shawl with the Italian blue thread running through it and drape it over her shoulders. It washes her face out, but she always insists on it. She'd ordered the wool from Milan and spent months crocheting it. She tucks it around her with her good hand and lets me wheel her back to my room. I pick up the scattered things and put them back in the drawers. There are also a number of boxes tipped over in the storage section of the closet. A broom lies beside them. I refill the boxes and pile them up. Mother obviously doesn't want anything here.

Returning to Mother's side, I ask, "Mother, what were you looking for?"

She looks up at me, eyes brighter than I've seen in years, and the normal side of her face working. The other side remains rigid. She grabs my hand, and places it open on her lap. Then she rummages around in her left pocket and pulls out a key strung on a crimson ribbon. She drops it into my hand. She'd found the key but not the container she wanted to open. I get a step-stool and climb up to get the wooden box off the closet shelf. It's not large, no bigger than a boot box, but she could never have got it down. Not even with the broom.

At one time, that box contained my father's important papers - will, insurance policy, and title to the farm - and when Kent and I moved Mother in, I'd popped it up there for safe-keeping thinking Mother's papers would also be in there.

When I place the box on Mother's knees, her eyes glow. After she makes several attempts to insert the key into the lock, I steady her hand with mine so she can manoeuvre it. Her hand seems so small and frail under mine. I can feel the bones. They're like cords barely holding together. The lock springs at last, but Mother doesn't open the box right away. She puts her hand on the top, surprisingly calm, and then slowly lifts it. She quickly closes it as if she's afraid something is going to jump out of it. After watching her do this a few times, I realize she's savouring the anticipation the same way I pour out my first glass of sparkling red wine, swish it around the glass, and take in the bouquet before tasting.

She opens it wide, gives me a fierce look and jerks her head toward the door. I back-step through it and busy myself in the kitchen. A cry, a howl really, brings me back to her side. She's holding a blue dress to her bosom. It has white daisies printed on it. The sight of the daisies so surprises me I can't console her. I just pull a chair up beside her and accept the dress when she hands it to me. One by one, she hands me the contents of the box: two pieces of broken Italian porcelain, one with the glass teardrop on it, the other displaying one side of an up-turned mouth; a letter signed Michel with train tickets attached, one adult, one child, to Milan, Italy; and a legal document. She watches me for some sign of understanding. Finally, she grabs the legal papers, opens them out, and points to the middle section. It's in italics and set off by a wide margin:

I, Dorothy Ann Billick, hereby retain custody
of Phyllis Marie by agreeing to stay
in my respective marriage to Fred Henry Billick.

On the line beneath it is Mother's signature, bolder than I've ever seen it.

Document in hand, I rock back and forth. Then I do something I haven't done in a long time; I meet my mother's olive green eyes, sunk deep into her pale, sagging face. And I talk to her about what I had seen in the wheat field so many years back. A sound develops in the back of her throat. It comes out of her mouth like a keening, the kind one hears from mothers at the graves of soldiers.

I take her hands in mine and hold them still. Smiling, I say, "Mom, do you remember the spilled milk in the carpet?" She nods. "I was the one who did it," I say.

The sound in her throat develops into a laugh. Not like the bubbly laugh of so long ago, but a laugh that's good enough for me. I lift her hands in the air, kick the brake on her chair and turn her round and round. We both laugh, timidly at first, then uproariously.

As I catch my breath, I look out the window at Fern and watch a gust of wind pick up her skirt and whip it around her stuffed body. Overhead, white clouds gather into long wisps, sweep westward across the cobalt sky and double back on themselves. A bright streak of blue and white cloth flashes beneath the clouds. Its Fern's scarf caught up in the same changing velocity.

Kent crosses this framed view of mine. He appears to be running after the scarf. When he catches it, I glance at Fern again, then down at myself, caught up in snug fitting jeans and a yellow sweater falling loosely over the swell of my breasts.

Shallow Water

Alecia thought him the perfect replacement. She liked the spring in his step and his compact leanness as she watched him run two Airedale terriers the length of Crescent Beach. She liked his hair blowing back from his face, outer strands sun-bleached a lighter blonde. And she liked his face. Clean-shaven. Wind-tanned. Square. Square, but without sharp angles at the chin. It softened there, made him look relaxed, easy-going.

Softness was important to Alecia. Her last man was hard. All angles. No matter how she shaped his moustache and beard, she could not soften the jut of his chin or the hard line of his mouth. And despite the various styles of shirts, jackets and sweaters she hauled out for him to try on, his shoulders, wide and square, had no more give in them than a drapery hanger.

She had only herself to blame, had purposely sought out an angular man. Angular men seemed more excitable. More willing to please.

Alecia could not see the blonde man's eyes. Eyes were of the essence. They would have to be uncluttered, blue perhaps. The last man's eyes were mysterious. At first, it seemed a good combination – an angular excitable man with mysterious brown eyes. But mysterious had come to mean surprise. Disorder. Alecia liked order.

Demerise, the tall, copper-haired protagonist in the novel Alecia was writing, also liked order. Demerise was married to an archaeologist who provided a home in the posh west side of Vancouver during the winter and travel to archaeological sites in the summer. This summer he was working feverishly to uncover Xeste 4, a three-storey building buried in 1500 B.C. at Akroteri, a site on the Greek Island, Santorini.

Demerise enjoyed preparing for these summers. She could co-ordinate air, train and boat travel, and locate rental property faster than her husband could gather equipment and organize students to accompany him. She was so fast that she would settle in and explore the new locale within a few weeks, and then have little to do the remainder of the summer.

Thus, while her husband crawled around pulling dirt away from the sides of ancient buildings or hills, Demerise organized affairs. She had already selected a lover for Santorini – a black-eyed Greek who owned a gleaming one-hundred foot yacht. Nothing could be more discreet.

Alecia could remember her own affairs. Even a time when she had almost married. It was in the '70's. He was a lawyer in a small town in New York. They lived in an old two-storey house that she decorated with decoupage and patterned wallpaper. To her friends, her life seemed cosy and destined for a top-storey condo in New York City with parties and benefits and a couple of kids to keep her company. But her lawyer began to buy things like edible bikini shorts and ordered her to comply. Alecia liked order, not being ordered.

After that, she tried to select her partners with greater care. First, she would query subtly: "On a road-trip with me, would you prefer stop-overs in country settings or in hotels equipped with everything from terry cloth bathrobes to adult T.V.?" If the thought of adult T.V. lit up their faces, she would take it further by steering them into love shops. A fifteen second fixation on edibles, videos, leather or chains would turn her into an instant sprinter.

Alecia's fate was to discard one man after the other. Each time, however, she tempered her disappointment with fantasy. Eventually, the men in her fantasies became so captivating that she totally gave in to them, assembling each one to suit a particular mood or period in her life. The last one was the angular man.

The angular man fit well into Alecia's summer fantasy. He would fetch her out of her poorly-lit apartment in Powell River and drive her to clean-smelling beaches. She preferred beaches that took a long time to reach, like Long Beach on Vancouver Island. There was the Little River ferry on which they would stand, bodies swaying in unison and hair streaming in the wind. There was the drive in the Miata, then the stop in Cathedral Grove where they would wind their arms around the Douglas Firs and try to touch one another's fingertips. There were the fingertips. And there was Long Beach where they would nestle behind huge pieces of driftwood, and the angular man, always delighted by the lack of undergarments beneath the peasant blouse and dirndl skirt she always wore would lower the blouse over her shoulders and slip his hand beneath her skirt. She would become wet and limp and wished that long drives and weekends on Vancouver Island could last forever.

Alecia's delight with her creation carried over to Demerise's world. Demerise was having the time of her life cruising the Aegean on the Greek's gleaming wooden yacht. The adventure was not only romantic, it was creative.

Each time she boarded the boat, the Greek greeted her in costume; tails at one point, a patch over one of his devilish eyes another, and once even in sandals and the loose-fitting chiton worn in ancient times.

And the boat was decked with a marble hot tub, plush blue towels and roses. Roses everywhere. In white vases on blue tablecloths. Lying across her pillow of sea blue silk. And in large vases of old Cycladic pottery. All red. Blood red.

Demerise became so heady from the experience that she would often confuse the two settings in which she lived. So far, however, her husband noticed nothing; his hands on her, rough and calloused from the volcanic ash, would jolt her back into the immediate setting just on time.

After a time, Alecia began to have doubts about her angular man. His eyes occasionally registered a desire for change. That was when she realized that mystery could turn into demand. Then, she worried about the angles; angles seemed to produce edginess. She had never been able to control demanding, edgy men. Although times had been good with him, she began to create another man. Not totally imaginative, she looked for a base from which to spring. The blonde man on Crescent Beach, looking so earthy in a hooded sweat shirt and rubber boots, was precisely what she required.

He was quite small. Blended into the expanse of ocean water surrounded by the Gulf Island, south, Point Grey, west, and the mountains of Vancouver, north, he looked even smaller. The sun bathed him, and everything around him, orange. Alecia was immediately drawn to the sun's pulsation toward the horizon. She knew it was an optical illusion but fell under its spell anyway.

As the sun slid closer and closer to the line of darkness, it increased in size, reddened and quickly disappeared. Alecia wondered if the sun's climax occurred when it rose or went down. Then she wondered if the blonde man liked making love in the morning or at night. She glanced over expecting to watch him throw the stick he had been carrying into the water for his terriers, but they had vanished. Like the sun. And damn it, she had not seen his eyes.

*

The Airedales first caught her attention. One loped toward a mongrel in a terra-cotta coat. The other ambled behind, water splattering his long, wiry hair. The blonde man, boots scrunching on the rocks, called out to the loping dog: "Maggie, come. Come. Maggie. MAGGIE. COME."

Alecia sat still on a log. She tried to study the rocks. They were interesting enough: jagged green and brown rocks, smooth rocks the same terra-cotta as the mongrel, pink, brown and best of all smooth rocks the colour and sheen of eggplant. She picked up one of the eggplants and turned it between her thumb and index finger.

As the air dried the stone, the lustre faded. This could be my symbol for the novel, she thought. Demerise's adventure with the Greek was becoming lack-lustre. Particularly in their parting. Often he was so occupied with the unloading of cargo that only his German shepherd dog was available to see her off the boat.

Maggie decided the hollow in Alecia's log was the perfect resting place. Alecia reached out to pet her, but quickly moved her hand back as the dog's neck fur rose to fine points.

"She won't hurt you," said a voice, gentle as the ocean spray that had just risen and misted Alecia's glasses. She wiped the mist away with her sleeve and looked up into a pair of eyes that were even gentler than the voice.

They were blue. Blue indeed. Comfortable. No questions in them. No hidden games. For the first time, Alecia felt like a cheat. She looked away hoping she had not yet transmitted the feeling from her eyes to his.

"I call her my holy terrier. Once in a while I let her off the leash, like Paddy here. But on occasion, she goes aggressive on me. I'm sorry if she startled you." The blonde man lifted his right foot onto the log and leaned forward to slip the leash into Maggie's collar. "I haven't seen you around here before."

"No. I'm just up for the weekend – a writer's seminar at Camp Alexandria."

"So, you're a writer. What do you write?"

"Fan…I mean fiction." Not wishing to go into detail she switched the attention to him. "What do you do?"

"I'm a photographer. Free-lance." His eyes scanned her face: the dark skin and high cheekbones; the long, thin nose and narrow lips. They settled again on her eyes, dark brown and wary.

In similar fashion, Alecia surveyed the blonde man's features, pressing each one into her memory: the forehead, wide with wisps of hair falling over it, the ruddy cheeks; the nose, broad but not out of proportion with his face; the bottom lip, full and sensuous. She ignored the slight downturn of his mouth. After all, she need not use all of him.

"You have an incredibly ethnic look. Do you mind if I ask your name?"

"No. It's Alecia."

"Alecia! That's precisely what your name should be. I hope you won't think this presumptuous of me, but may I photograph you? You have great bone structure. I could do you justice. What do you say? We could do it around five o'clock when the shadows are at their best."

Although Alecia's lips shaped themselves into a NO, she nodded. It was the smile that did it. It stretched that full lip wide exposing every line and tiny wind-dried crack. It looked so vulnerable that she wanted to touch it with her finger. With her lip. With her tongue. She wanted to feel the accompanying flutter that would course straight to her groin. She had never completely achieved that with her angular man.

*

At four-forty-five Alecia climbed onto a smooth black rock and watched a group of seagulls gather. They were so raucous she did not hear the blonde man approach. And despite the fact that she expected him, she jumped when he touched her shoulder.

"My dogs and I have a way of startling you, don't we?"

Alecia nodded. She hoped the turmoil she was experiencing inside could not be observed from the outside.

"This is excellent. See. The sun isn't too high. Look at that seagull – highlighted – and its shadow – exaggerated. That's the effect we'll get with you."

A warning went off in Alecia's head. This man is too enthusiastic.

"I've got a terrific idea."

Here it comes.

"That is if you're adventurous enough to do it."

Stop him.

Alecia began to protest, but it was too late.

"The best photo I've ever seen was of a woman lying on her stomach in shallow water. We could go one up on it with this side lighting. Also, if you were to lie there for a while, I'll bet the birds would come up close. I could spread crumbs around you. On your stomach. We could get the shot of the century with a little patience."

Order, thought Alecia, I like order. Birds clawing me and plopping on me, not to mention walking back to camp in cold, wet clothes are not my idea of order.

"I thought you were interested in my bone structure."

"You bet I am. You could prop your face in your hands and angle your head toward the camera. And look, I've brought you a blouse to enhance your bone structure."

He turned a plastic bag upside down in her lap. Alecia unfolded the white garment, held it up against her chest and giggled self-consciously. It was scooped round and decorated with red crisscross embroidery which gathered on a draw string. Unable to resist, she slipped it on and tucked it into the waist of her faded blue jeans.

The blonde man smiled, his bottom lip quivering a little. He looked straight into her eyes and asked, "Well, how about it?"

Demerise, Alecia thought. What would Demerise do? But she quickly realized panic was leading her to the ridiculous.

Demerise liked order, but only to give her time for chaos. Why, Demerise would immediately slip the blouse off her right shoulder, throw her copper mane to the left and lie in the water as if she belonged there. And afterwards, she would help herself to that bottom lip.

Alecia cast her eyes about for an alternate solution. The magnolia trees? No. He would want them in bloom. The seagulls on a rock, one standing, the other sitting? No. They looked too much like gift-shop replicas. The clam-digger? Yes. Now all she would have to do is match the blonde man's enthusiasm.

"Look. We could borrow that man's apparatus and take sequence shots of clam-digging. I bet he'd let us if we include him in some of the photos."

Well aware of the long-shot he'd played, the blonde man picked up his camera and tripod and began walking toward the clam digger. Alecia followed, wondering suddenly what this blonde man's name was. She tried a few on him – Kenneth, Peter, Michael, perhaps T.J. – but checked herself. If she thought about it long enough, she would surely ask him and it was better to leave her men nameless. Names seemed too personal somehow. Harder to discard. And see how easy it was to leave the angular man and take up this blonde man.

After numerous poses - active: biting the cylindrical apparatus into the sand and twisting the handle on top; inactive: resting for a moment, face tilted to the camera; active: sand spewing all directions and Alecia standing back, arms stretched out in front; inactive: the clam catch on the end of the auger, Alecia smiling triumphantly; active: removing the clam; with man; with dog; with man and dog and many clams; and alone, face silhouetted against the darkening sky – the blonde man was satisfied.

Alecia felt a little like a model, at least what she thought it must be like. For the first time in her life, her body did not seem detached from her. Nor did her limbs hang separate from her trunk. She felt like one organism, whole and fluid. The sensation was so good she wanted to take the blonde man's hands and swing him around in a circle. She wanted to pull him down to his knees and cup his face in her hands. She wanted to taste that bottom lip.

"Well, so long, Alecia." The blonde man was snapping his camera case shut and had already folded the tripod.

"Wait. I'll walk as far as the camp with you. Here, let me untie Maggie and take her for you." Alecia reached for the leash and accidentally brushed the blonde man's leg. She pulled her hand back and looked up at him. It was in his eyes too. She was sure of it.

A sound began to develop in his throat, but was drowned out by a group of seagulls chortling at one another and a crow cawing loudly from his perch on a tall thin rock. Alecia noticed a long-necked bird walking through a puddle of water, a lone species amongst the grey and white squawkers. I'm that bird, she thought, as she walked and listened to the blonde man speak of his grandparents. How they were two of the first settlers on Crescent Beach. How his grandfather had emulated the tropics in his back yard to make his Hawaiian war-bride feel at home.

"I would think that a bit tough."

"She had to settle for cedar trees instead of coconut palms and Virginia Creepers for philodendron, but the yard is remarkable, Alecia. My grandfather hauled in two tons of rock and built a cove with a spring-fed pool nestled inside. The water trickles down the rocks into the pool and because of the moisture ferns grow naturally out of the crevices. My grandmother used to swim in the pool as spryly as a young girl. Do you know what she'd do first?"

Alecia shook her head.

"She'd pick a Ti leaf from the garden and throw it into the pool. If it floated, she proclaimed the pool safe from the sea monster."

"This is from an old legend, I presume."

"Yes. A floating Ti leaf meant the monster was away from his lair."

"Did one ever sink?"

"No. But the thought of a monster in the depths of the pool certainly sparked my imagination. I used so many Ti leaves that Grandmother had to increase the number of plants she grew. She used to start them in the house and Grandfather would transplant them in the garden in May or so. Actually, he brought out all her tropical plants and mixed them with the indigenous flowers. I still have a hibiscus grown from clippings off the original plant. I kept it because Grandmother always wore an orange one in her hair. In fact, when the monster failed to appear, I decided Grandmother held some kind of extra charm that was connected to that flower."

"You seem awfully connected to your grandparents. Did they raise you?"

"No. If they had, I probably wouldn't have been so charmed."

"But you live there now, don't you?"

"Yes. They willed their property to me. I guess my interest in them and their history gave them reason to believe I'd maintain it. They were so devoted to one another. I'd like to emulate that with someone some day. So far, unfortunately, my devotion has been to upkeep. I just re-finished the hardwood this past winter. This summer, I intend to solidify the rocks in the cove and perhaps weave a hammock so as to preserve the one Grandfather imported."

Alecia wanted to pinch herself to determine whether or not she was in one of her fantasies. Or fictions. This man was too good to be real. If he was real, she wanted him. Body. Name. Soul.

The blonde man's voice broke into her thoughts: "Well, Alecia, here we are at your Camp. Thank you for posing on the beach." He tapped his camera. "I won't forget you." He took Maggie's leash from her, put it in the same hand as Paddy's and reached out to push back the hair that had loosened from her braid. "You may keep the blouse. I don't think it could suit anyone else better."

Alecia's hands flew to her bodice. She had forgotten she was wearing it. She opened her mouth to ask him if she could accompany him home for tea or coffee, or just to see his back yard, but Maggie yanked at the leash and it slipped out of his hand. The blonde man took off after her, full tilt, Paddy loping alongside. Alecia took a few steps toward them, and then ran around a corner in hope of catching up with them. But they had vanished.

Alecia touched her face where the blonde man had picked up the strands of hair. She fingered the area above her ear where she would normally pin a red rose. It was hard to imagine a switch to hibiscus. Hibiscus flowers were so large and unruly in comparison.

A soft, blonde man. She would have to make him more respectable, though. Perhaps cut his hair a few inches and give him a moustache – just a thin one, so as not to over-power that bottom lip. And she would have to do something about his requests. Lie in the water, indeed! She couldn't decide, however, what to do with the dogs; sloppy as they were, they added a certain character.

DISTURBANCES

I am the bones named Kala Wakaw. That isn't my real name, but Deirdre Dubois, the woman who found me and named me, has no idea who I am. I came to life, so to speak, a few days ago when Deirdre's friend, Reinhart Schmidt, dug part of me up with the shovel of his back-hoe. It was my skull, ochre in colour. It rolled down the hill he'd gouged and settled at Deirdre's boot-clad feet. I gazed through the holes that were my eyes at the leather laces wound around dozens of hooks on her boots, and then up at her face. She began to scream.

That was our introduction. I meant no harm. Eventually, she calmed and picked up my skull. She held it as if it were going to bite or explode in her hands.

"It's just a pumpkin," Reinhart yelled, as he lowered the back-hoe scoop to violate the rest of my hill. What he'd already dug up looked like an open wound.

Deirdre transferred my skull to one hand and held up the other, palm out, to stop Reinhart. She gingerly returned her hand beneath me as he braked and jumped off the machine.

"I'll be darned," Reinhart said, taking my skull from her. He held it firmly and turned it round and round to peer into all my openings.

Now that she didn't have to touch me, Deirdre's curiousity piqued. "Why is it orange?" she asked.

I could have put the answer in her head, but Reinhart barged in with an explanation: "Probably iron oxide in the soil." He traced each side of my face with his index finger and ran it across my teeth, hesitating at the crooked ones on top. "There's no dental work," he said. "This skull is old."

Actually, I'm one hundred and eleven years old counting the twenty-five years before my burial. I died in 1918 when the flu swept through the country. You'd think I and my people would've suffered enough coming to this lonely land of brush and sloughs and blood-sucking horseflies and mosquitoes. You'd think near starvation and frost-bite which brought us to the brink of death would have been sufficient.

But, that's enough about me for now. My voice has been silenced for many years, and I've grown to accept that. This story's mainly about Deirdre whose voice has also been silenced. Her voice is in her hands. She models objects from the very thing I reside in, clay. But since her husband Jacques' death, her hands have been still. She orders clay, but when it arrives and she slices off a portion to knead, her fingers stiffen and the clay falls to table or floor. The loss of Jacques seems to have wrung everything out of her.

That's why she hired Reinhart and his back-hoe to dig into my hill. She's hoping the construction of an old-fashioned wood-burning kiln, partially embedded in my hill, will bring back her passion to create. I've heard her tell Reinhart one just like it had helped her great grandmother, Kalynka Budnyk, return to sculpting after the son she'd carried for the full nine months died during delivery. It wasn't until her grandmother saw what beauty could be brought out of ashes that she could erase the image she'd conjured up of her little one becoming ash. In Deirdre's situation, she wants to see that beauty quickly, to erase the sinking feeling she experiences each time she thinks of Jacques' ashes falling through her fingers into the North Saskatchewan River. He'd requested this ritual because he'd canoed the river when he was young and vibrant and free. Release for him. Anguish for her. He was gone forever. She'd rather imagine his bones buried nearby, like mine, where she could at least visit him.

As for my skull, Reinhart seemed at home with it in his hands. He traced around each one of my teeth. Even Deirdre reached out and ran her little finger across my teeth. "How old do you think it is?" she asked.

"A hundred, maybe. It would have taken that long for her to turn such a deep orange."

Deirdre's eyes shot up to Reinhart. "Her?"

"Yes. The teeth are smaller than a man's would be." He moved his fingers to my brow and slid them toward my cranium. "And the forehead is rounder."

"How do you know all this?" she asked.

"I grew up around things like this," he answered. "My father was a museum curator. You wouldn't believe how many unidentified skulls and bones get stored in archives."

"Of whom?"

"Europeans and Africans,"

Deirdre's brows furrowed.

Reinhart settled my skull in the palm of his right hand and glanced skyward. "That was in Germany, Deirdre," he said. "I lived there until my mother died of tuberculoses. Papa couldn't bear up, so we emigrated."

"Did he find work in museums here?" Deirdre asked.

"No," Reinhart said. He looked down at my skull and tapped the top of it with his left forefinger. "He couldn't work around items like this without thinking of my mother being reduced to a set of bones in her grave. So Papa's uncle sponsored us and hired Papa to work on his farm. Eventually, Papa took it over. He couldn't get away from his previous work entirely, though. Almost every time he broke a new piece of bushed land he'd find bones. I was often on the machinery with him, so it was natural for me to be curious. Later, I took anthropology courses at University. It seemed destined."

"University?" Deirdre said, raising her eyebrows again and glancing at the backhoe.

"I majored in Accounting, but couldn't stand desk work." Reinhart smiled and met Deirdre's eyes for a few seconds. I noticed that Reinhart's eyes were a pure blue, like cornflowers, and Deirdre's the dark brown colour of black-eyed-Susans.

Deirdre nodded. "I guess I can understand that. I majored in Creative Writing, but couldn't sit still long enough to produce a body of work."

She took my skull from him and placed it on a flat rock. It was amongst a number of rocks Reinhart had shoved down the hill. My grave is shallow, so rocks had been placed on top to keep foxes, weasels and coyotes from digging me up.

Deirdre looked at my skull, sitting so prim, for several seconds. She glanced up to the excavated area and swept her hand toward it. "Reinhart, do you think there are more bones in there?" she asked.

"There's only one way to find out," he said. "Do you have any garden trowels?"

Deirdre nodded and walked over to the garden shed.

I cringed.

She produced two trowels.

As they walked up the hill, trowels in hand, Reinhart asked, "Did you notice where I dislodged the skull?" Deirdre shook her head, but soon found the hollow my skull left. She bent down and shoved her trowel into the earth near my neck bones. Reinhart grabbed her hand. "Carefully, Deirdre," he said. "And if the trowel touches something solid, dig it out bit by bit with your hands." She slowed down and delicately slid the implement into the ground.

"Odd they'd put the body in a hill," Deirdre said, biting her lip as she placed the earth above the hollow.

"Maybe it was a native custom," Reinhart said.

Deirdre stopped digging. "You think it's native, Reinhart?"

"Who else? The settlers all used cemeteries of a sort. They all came with some kind of European religion. Often, they came here because of religious persecution." He glanced at Deirdre's boots. "Maybe it's one of your ancestors." A grin spread across his sun-scorched face.

Earlier, he'd teased Deirdre about wearing her knee-high moccasin-style boots in such hot weather. She'd told him her great-grandmother, who had married a Plains Ojibwa man and adopted some of his customs, always wore boots like that when embarking on new ventures. She'd unlaced the boots to show him how her great grandmother used to do it, both cords in one hand and a quick wind around the hooks.

Deirdre tried to return Reinhart's smile. It came out as a twitch on the right side of her mouth. She looked down and busied herself with the earth above my rib cage. "*Baba* said her boots gave her good luck," she said.

"Was the good luck part a native custom?" Reinhart asked.

"I don't know," she answered, glancing back up at him. "It could have come from her Slavic background. I just like to tap into my Grandmother's intuition before I do anything. As you know, she worked with clay, too."

I'm afraid I haven't a speck of Indian blood in me. I came to this country because my parents dragged me from my relatives and friends in the Ukraine to flee the brutal Austrians and Hungarians who had occupied our country. And I was buried here because my family was sick, too, and couldn't take me to a burial ground. They could hardly drag themselves out to dig my grave.

My real name is Elena Bukascz. I was seven years old when my family journeyed to Halifax by boat and to Saskatchewan by train. We thought our pregnant mother was going to die from seasickness on the boat. My father walked the decks crying. He thought he was going to be left alone with four children. It took six weeks to reach an immigration house and a few more days to reach our homestead in a wagon pulled by oxen. We were bone-weary and down-hearted. We'd transported ourselves from a village full of homes and people to a stubborn land in stark wilderness. Our first winter, we huddled in a *burdei* which my father built by digging a hole, stretching logs over it and covering it with sod.

All of a sudden, Reinhart's trowel touched my pelvic bone. He put it down and began moving the earth with his hands. Within minutes, his hands were curving around my pelvis and he was letting out a triumphant shout: "It's a female all right."

To Deirdre's questioning look, he added, "It's wider than a male's. But even more tell-tale is this." He pointed to the tiny skull of my second child which was lodged in the bottom cavity of my pelvis. I had been seven months along when I became ill.

Deirdre glanced at it and looked away. "Reinhart, this feels terribly invasive," she said, "like we're stripping someone naked. I don't think we should be doing this." She picked up both trowels.

Reinhart lifted my pelvic bone from its hollow, careful not to disturb my little one, and carried it to the rock where my skull had been placed. He set it down beside my skull. Then, he sat down on the ground beside the rock and studied Deirdre's hesitant face. "Do you want to call someone in?" he asked.

She shrugged. "Maybe."

He stood up and turned toward his truck. "I'll get a box just in case."

While he searched for a suitable container, Deirdre left the digging area and paced up and down the weedy yard. She stopped finally, crouched down and touched the earth in an effort to grasp what owning this land meant to her. She pulled out some of the quack grass and studied the roots. They were dry. Rain hadn't fallen in several weeks. It was ten o'clock in the morning, but the temperature had already picked up to around 25 celcius, unusually high for the area. All the plants Reinhart had dug up lay wilted in the dirt piled next to the rock on which my bones sat. Deirdre gathered some of them up and examined their roots also. She looked down at my bones and placed the plants beside me. Then, she bent down, unwound the cords on her boots, removed them and stood them beside my skull. She stood back and gazed at the arrangement.

When Reinhart returned, Deirdre picked up my skull to place in the box. She lowered it to the bottom and then lifted it back out, turned away and walked barefoot down to the lakeshore. Her hands throbbed around my skull as she stood there observing the east to west flow of the lake water. She related it to how blood once flowed around my skull and pelvic bone. The words *life force* entered her mind. Jacques' face appeared and she thought of the blood that used to flow through his veins. She imagined her own blood flowing through the veins in her body and reminded herself of how easily it can stop. She wondered how *she* would feel if she were one day unearthed from *her* resting place. Would she feel exposed, violated?

Deirdre looked down at my skull and cradled it to her bosom. She walked slowly back to Reinhart holding my skull high in her hands. "Let's name her Wakaw, after the lake," she said. The gold pigment in her eyes lit up slightly. "And Kala, after Kalynka, my great grandmother. And let's put her back where she belongs."

She composed a mental image of what I might have looked like in life: a spirited young woman, tall and lanky, who wore her hair away from her forehead and straight down her back. She dressed me in loose buckskin clothes to cover my bulging abdomen and pulled boots decorated with various colours of beads onto my feet.

In truth, I was stocky and earthy-looking with a wide homely face. My blonde hair had been cropped for easy removal of nits. My clothes were ill-fitted garments made from flour sacks. But never mind, I rather liked my new image.

The name bothered me some, though, as it would anyone, identity being one's essence. I thought about it: Kalynka. Slavic. Like me. And Wakaw, Cree for "crooked," like my teeth and back. I supposed I'd get used to it.

Deirdre lowered her arms, shifted my skull into her right hand and traced each dip and contour of it with the fingers of her left hand. Then, she carried it back up the hill and placed it in the rounded out section from which I'd been dislodged. She knelt down and filled my skull with particles of dirt. With each sifting of soil, she mentally blessed me and apologized for the disturbance. Reinhart followed suit with my pelvis. Together, they hand shoveled the remaining topsoil that had been excavated onto my grave and the surrounding area.

We'd better find some plants to replace the ones we tore out," Reinhart said. "Some sage. And roses. And chamomile."

I rejoiced, even though he forgot crocuses and tiger lilies.

Deirdre knelt down beside me and patted the earth firmly over my bones. She rocked back and forth several times before she looked down at her hands and noticed how much dirt there was in the creases and beneath her nails. She got up and walked to the house where she filled the bathroom sink with warm soapy water and attacked her nails with a stiff brush. As she scrubbed, it occurred to her that she may be washing her hands of something she shouldn't be. She wondered if I'd be happier having my ancestry determined and a proper burial in a like cemetery. She questioned her own comfort in the constant presence of my bones. Aloud, she said, "Am I playing God?"

She turned on the hot water tap and placed her hands under the steamy stream. When they turned a bright red, she pulled them away. She dried her hands on a faded brown towel and glanced up and into the mirror over the sink. She saw a woman of forty years who looked fifty. The long, thick, chestnut-coloured hair she'd worn loose was now sprinkled with gray and pulled straight back and tied with a leather cord. The face that had once shined with pink health was ashen. And the gold-flecked brown eyes which used to glow like gems were dull and hollow. She peered closer and saw that the veins in her temples throbbed. She reached up to massage them, but changed her mind and lowered her hands to her rounded abdomen.

"Jacques knew about Marc," she whispered to her swollen image in the mirror. She turned on the hot water tap again and shoved her hands beneath.

From what I've gathered listening to Deirdre rave in the back yard, Marc became Jacques' home care nurse when the Lou Gehrig's disease began to cripple him. Marc was apparently a strong, good-looking man whose voice was so gentle and kind she felt weak to the core whenever he spoke. O-oh, how the body can rule. Even I, in all my shyness, might have been lured away from Nicholas, by Emil, our new neighbour from Hungary, if I'd succumbed to the invitation in his eyes. Especially during that bad patch Nick had after being caught and jailed for making and selling home-brew in the bushes behind here.

Deirdre removed her hands from her abdomen and lifted them to her temples. As she circled them with her index and middle fingers, she caught her image in the mirror again, noticing that her clothes, a loose sepia coloured blouse and a long brown elasticized skirt were stretched to the limit. She hadn't yet shopped for maternity clothes. She also saw that her shoulders were sagging some, especially the right one, and lamented the fact that she'd become as slow as an elephant and was only five months along. "A far cry," she muttered, "from the words graceful and cat-like people used to describe me as." She looked at the down-turn of her mouth and tried to smile. It resembled a grimace. It reminded her of Jacques' emaciated face as the Lou Gehrig's disease slowly overtook him. "I'm dying, too," she said into the mirror. She wondered whether she'd meet Jacques in the afterlife and be able to tell him how sorry she was and how much she missed him and loved him, would always love him, only him. She hadn't said these things to him at the end because he'd been unconscious. It was only later that she learned the last thing to leave a person is hearing.

Her left hand crept back to the hot water tap. She glanced down at her hand as if it were apart from herself then jerked it back up. She grabbed the brown towel off the wall dowel, stomped out to her porch and spread it over the broken slats on a wooden chair.

The chair had come with the old weathered house. As she sat down, she looked at the tear in the screen door, the spaces around the windows, and the yard in which every building appeared ready to fall down and every flower bed was overgrown with weeds. "What have I done?" she whispered, covering her face with her red, water-crinkled hands.

Reinhart, bless his heart, appeared right then with a bouquet of freshly picked black-eyed-Susans and a pail full of clay which he'd retrieved from my hill. Deirdre acknowledged them with a nod and forced herself to take her hands away from her face and place them in her lap. She rubbed her fingers while Reinhart pulled a chair up beside her. As he sat down, she noticed a twitch in his nose. Voice weary, she asked, "What is it, Reinhart?"

He took a deep breath. "This property may have been an Indian burial site, Deirdre."

Her head snapped back. "Don't tell me that."

"That's exactly what I'm telling you. I think we should avoid any more digging. We could build a free-standing electric kiln instead. I'm more familiar with them and they're much cleaner and easier to use. It would also eliminate the need for a damper and a flue."

"But I had my heart set on wood firing, Reinhart. It creates a glow you can't get with other kilns. Glow and shadow. And unique combinations of colour."

"Yeah, I've looked it up," Reinhart said, pointing to the shelf of books Deirdre had set up on the side wall of her porch. "No oxygen, so the fired wood zaps it out of the oxides in the clay and glaze. Perhaps we could try a beehive kiln. Or a pit kiln. They both use wood."

A look of disappointment crossed Deirdre's face. Her body slumped. "But, I so wanted it to be just like *Baba*'s."

Deciding to abandon the argument for the moment, Reinhart reached into the pail, scooped up some of the clay and placed it in Deirdre's hands. She balanced it in one hand, then the other, noting he'd added water and worked it in for her just as he used to do for his wife, Cassandra.

From what I've been able to gather, Reinhart builds kilns because he first built one for Cassandra, and then went on to building a number of them for other potters in the area. Cassandra's no longer around. Apparently, an urge to experience the vibrations of the ocean in order to transfer them to her art had been so irresistible she packed up her wheel, clay and tools and moved to Salt Spring Island in B.C. Reinhart stayed behind, and now time seems to have shouldered its way into whatever was left of their relationship.

Deirdre shifted the clay from hand to hand then rolled it into a ball. She broke a piece off, formed a coil and wrapped it around her index finger. She examined it for cracks, saw there weren't any, a good sign, and set it aside to dry. "When it's dry we can check for alkaline content," she said. She got up, searched the cupboard against the back wall and pulled out a pair of rubber gloves and a bottle of hydrochloric acid. When she saw Reinhart's look of warning, she informed him it had been diluted with water. She pinched a bit of clay off the coil and dropped it into the acid mixture. She watched for bubbles and when there weren't any determined the clay free of lime. "This clay may be usable," she said, "as long as it doesn't turn white from alkali." She sat back down in her chair, removed the coil from her finger and handed it to Reinhart. "We'll still need to have it tested to find out what temperature it will vitrify at." She didn't lift her eyes from the clay and, so far, everything she did and said seemed rote.

Reinhart fingered the clay, squeezing it to lengthen it. He wrapped it around his wrist twice. "If this looks good when it's dry," he said, "I'll make a tile and take it over to Cassandra's old kiln. The person who bought it will be firing her pieces any day now. She says she'll need a fairly high temperature because she's been experimenting with local clay also."

Deirdre nodded, re-formed the left-over clay into a ball and threw it back into the pail. She drummed her fingers on the arms of the chair. "Maybe I don't need a kiln," she said. "Maybe I need a new career."

Until Jacques' illness, Deirdre had practiced many forms of clay work, from mask-making to vessels to free-form pieces. She particularly loved free form, but of late she'd found herself only able to manage the mask-making. She relied on masks for the major part of her income. Fortunately, their construction had always been second nature to her, having learned it from her great grandmother as a child. I've overheard her telling Reinhart how she'd lie down on a white sheet in her grandmother's back yard with a straw in her mouth while her grandmother smeared Vaseline over her face and under her chin and laid strips of wet plaster – the kind used in casts for broken legs or arms – over top. The straw would allow her to breathe while her grandmother worked. She'd loved the feel of the cold wet plaster strips being smoothed over her bone structure. As it dried, the plaster had become tighter and tighter against her skin until she'd thought her skin would pull away with the mask when her grandmother removed it.

At one time, Deirdre owned a mask for each year of her childhood. She'd enjoyed feeling her own development under her fingers; the shape of her face changing from baby round to oval, and her fat cheeks eventually releasing the kind of high bones a photographer would salivate over. Unfortunately, all but the original mask disintegrated over time. Her grandmother preserved the original by placing it on a plate stand inside an old glass case that had been handed down to her by her grandmother. Deirdre still had that case and mask sitting on the fireplace mantle. Although she'd always treasured it, she hadn't realized the significance of it until seeing the death masks of Royals in Italian museums. Preservation of a loved ones' face for ever more. Their masks, however, weren't made of lowly plaster, but of alabaster and marble. She wished Jacques had let her make a mask of his face. She'd tried once, but the plaster made him feel like he was smothering.

Reinhart, forever curious about origins, had wanted to know what made Deirdre decide to try her hand at making masks out of clay.

"After my grandmother died, I made a mould of her face, just as the Italians did," she told him, " but instead of leaving it pure white, I decided to use it as a mould for clay. It seemed appropriate to preserve her with the material she worked in. When I pulled it out of the kiln, it occurred to me that I could do this for people who were alive. They wouldn't be sombre like *Baba's*, though; they'd be fun and whimsical." Apparently she accomplished this by familiarizing herself with her customer's lifestyles and tastes, and then etching the masks to suit them. Once fired, she added complimentary items like beads, bits of coloured fabrics and papers, feathers and furs.

Sitting there, on the porch with Reinhart, she thought about the dozen moulds she had ready to be cast. She only had enough clay for half of them. If the clay Reinhart found resisted melting in the heat of Cassandra's kiln she'd be able to knead it and form 3/8" slabs to place over the moulds and carefully press into them. Then, all it would take to complete the raw forms would be to stuff them with bunched up plastic, place a board over them and turn them over for removal from the mould. The plastic would be a preventative measure to keep the masks from caving in when lifting them off the moulds.

Deirdre had the frame of mind to do all this because it was a step by step procedure. As for finishing them, she wasn't at all sure she could think whimsically enough. Whimsy didn't seem to belong in Deirdre's vocabulary anymore. Too much reality had been added to the substance of her life. She'd seen illness at its ugliest and watched death creep into Jacques' body, withering it to bones covered with paper thin skin. She'd known loneliness in its darkest sense, a face next to hers which couldn't make a sound or even an expression any more. She'd also known the depth of despair looking into a pair of sunken eyes which appealed for help she couldn't give. And now, she was sick with pregnancy, had very little income and couldn't settle down to work.

She was still hanging on to the word talent, but feared it wouldn't be long before it, too, would vanish. Even the masks required a certain amount of it. The fear burrowed deep into her brain and spread throughout her body until she could feel it in the marrow of her bones.

And without it, what would she do? She had no other talents. No training. And soon she'd have a baby to care for.

She hadn't called on Marc for help, or even told him about the pregnancy; neither of them had conceived this child out of an act of love. It was pure lust sparked by a touch of hands and a meeting of eyes. Besides, she was years older and he was married. I've listened to all this in her back yard ravings. "Once and I get caught," she has screamed. She has also ranted about thinking she was experiencing early menopause. Was she referring to change of life? The curse one month and not the next?

If that's it, I could see why she didn't use a knitting needle or hurl herself down the stairs she'd so willingly descended with Marc. Apparently, that was the only staircase that hadn't been converted into a wheelchair ramp and they'd thought it safe enough from Jacques' probing eyes. Ha! If Jacques had probing eyes he probably picked it up long before they actually did it.

Would you believe she thought the nausea had been brought on by the grief? The things we talk ourselves into. I'd thought my pregnancy was causing my illness and kept on trying to nurse my family.

Deirdre was in a fine mess. I wondered what I could do to help her.

*

It comes to me a week after I'd been disturbed. When I see her sitting by the lakeshore, water lapping over her feet. I quickly will her to look at the water. "No idleness in this water," I whisper. I then direct her attention to the flutter of the leaves on the poplar trees lining each side of her property and the tall grasses and reeds caught up in the wind's momentum. "Now, look at yourself," I say. "You're still as a door knob, only turning when Reinhart has a hand on you. What will you do when he's not here?"

She looks at everything I pointed out, but not at length like I'd hoped. And she totally ignores all of it, getting up instead and heading back to that dratted wooden chair. There, she sits down and closes her eyes as if to shut me out. Eventually, she drifts into a deep sleep.

Fiddlesticks! Now what? Jacques? Maybe he could wake her up. I call on him.

"She's pregnant with another man's child," he says. "Why should I?"

"Because she nursed you, fool," I say. "Because she loves you and gave up a lot for you. And because she feels guilty and may never live comfortably again if you don't intervene. Besides, who's the one who left her penniless with those copper penny stock purchases?"

That's a low blow, but what else can I resort to?

"She had the house," he says, a defiant look on his face.

"Yes," I say, "with leans on it. All she could afford was this broken down place."

"All right, all right," he says, agitated by the fact that there are no secrets among the dead. He makes an effort though, by shaving and putting on a clean royal blue shirt, Deirdre's favourite colour on him. He ambles into the yard and walks up the three-step entry to the porch.

I whisper, "Wake her up."

He puts his hand on her shoulder. She slumbers on. I motion to him to shake her shoulder. She awakens, but is too sleepy to open her eyes. Jacques backs toward the steps.

Sensing him there, Deirdre cries out: "No. Come back." But the words don't come out aloud. She tries again, but again the words catch in her throat. She reaches out for him. He hesitates then comes closer. He bends toward her. Deirdre tries to slip her right hand into one of his. He ignores her hand and looks at the rise on her belly. A look of disgust spreads across his face. He straightens, turns around and heads for the steps. She calls out his name, aloud this time, but he disappears.

So much for that idea! I'd hoped he'd reached a dimension big enough to forgive. I guess we'll have to leave that alone for a while. Perhaps I'd better go back to getting the woman working. It won't be easy. Deirdre looks as if she'd been into some of Nick's home brew. Her eyes only open half-way. She tears at her hands with her nails, the way she used to when suffering from eczema as a child, and then picks up the clay and rubs her fingers with it. It doesn't relieve the irritation, giving her a new fear that the eczema has returned and will render her hands useless in clay. She throws the dark grey lump back into the pail, stands up, stuffs her hands in her skirt pockets and walks into the parched yard. She looks west across the water and watches the sun sinking into the horizon. It's as orange as my skull. Its reflection trails in the lake water. A figure in a canoe crosses the reflection. It paddles to shore and pulls in beside her dock. She looks around for Reinhart, but he has gone. When she glances back to the dock she sees no one, not even the canoe. She scans the banks lining the lake. No sign of life other than the ducks and geese swimming lazily below them. She goes inside, switches on the kitchen light, twists the sink tap open and shoves a white porcelain kettle under the stream of water. As she reaches for the clay tea canister under the window, she catches a glimpse of someone running across the yard.

Uneasy, she drags the cinnamon-coloured stuffed chairs she'd bought at a garage sale to the doors. She hadn't been prudent enough to outfit the doors with dead bolts. With the knobs positioned just above the middle of the chairs, she tests them to see how difficult it would be to push them open. Too easy. She pushes them aside and drags two bureaus to the doors. It's hard work and she sinks into a chair afterward, conscious of the fact that she shouldn't be straining like this.

When rested, she gets up and fetches two sleeping pills. She goes to bed without bothering to fix herself a meal or make the cup of tea she'd begun. The pills, I've noticed, are her refuge, her wall between herself and the anguish of grief and guilt. I worry she'll take too many one of these days.

In the morning, Deirdre awakes to heavy pounding on the door, and then a face peering into her bedroom window. She screams and flies out of bed grabbing the telephone and a robe the colour of dried blood.

A quiet, calm voice says, "It's me, Reinhart. Put the phone down."

"Oh, God," she says, sinking to the bed in relief.

When she pushes the bureau aside at the back door and lets him in, he asks, "What's going on? Are you okay?"

"No. Yes. Oh, God." Deirdre covers her face with her hands. "I got a terrible fright last night." She bursts into tears.

Reinhart pushes the bureau back in place and pours water for coffee. While Deirdre explains her blockade, he carefully measures the grounds with a tablespoon and slowly empties each one into the top portion of a dented aluminum percolator, another garage sale item. He turns to Deirdre and points the spoon at her. "You need a man around here," he says. "How about I stay with you for a few days?" He flexes the bicep in his right arm and looks out the window.

Deirdre flinches. "I can take care of myself, Reinhart," she says. "Besides, in a few days you'll be finished the kiln and I'll be on my own anyway."

Good. Deirdre and I have work to do and I can't work with a man around. I never could. My work always seemed trivial in the face of all Nicholas had to do.

Mid-morning, Reinhart drives off to Wakaw to fetch the used fire bricks he'd negotiated a deal on. Deirdre, I see, is holding fast to her plan for a wood-burning kiln. Once his half-ton truck is out of sight, she visits me and once again mumbles apologies for disturbing me. She kneels when she speaks to me. I'm thinking of how fond of her I'm becoming when Joshua walks into the yard.

"You leave those bones in that hill," he says. Deirdre jerks around to find herself face to face with good old wizened Joshua, brown as a hazelnut and as hard as one.

"Bones?" Deirdre says, when she recovers from the intrusion.

"The bones of that woman you're sitting beside. She'll be ours."

Deirdre feigns puzzlement: "Ours?"

Joshua breathes out through his nose. "The Cree Indians. We were here long before you Europeans came."

Deirdre stands up, her height giving her an advantage over this determined little man. "What makes you think someone was buried here?" she asks.

He sweeps his right hand in an all-encompassing manner. "I watch everything goes on around here," he says. "And, lady, don't you dare give those bones to the government. We'll never get them back."

"Are you the one I saw in a canoe on the beach last night?" Deirdre asks.

He grins exposing his lack of front teeth. "Likely," he says.

Deirdre places both of her hands on the round of her abdomen. "You scared me half to death when you ran across my yard. That's not good for someone in my condition."

Joshua's eyebrows lift.

Deirdre touches my grave. "The skeleton in here pregnant, too," she says.

Joshua takes a step toward my grave and asks, "What are you planning to do with her?"

"Leave her there," Deirdre says. "She's been there a long time. I don't think she wants her bones, or her child's bones, moved."

"She wouldn't like sharing her property with a Caucasian," Joshua says, stressing the first syllable so that the word sounds more suitable for a crow than a person.

"She shared it with the previous owners," Deirdre says, turning her eyes toward Joshua and allowing them to penetrate his. I see she possesses power in those eyes.

He holds his eyes steady with hers and says, "Yes, but they didn't know she was here."

"Did you know?" she asks.

"No," he answers. "But I'm not surprised."

A stubborn look crosses Deirdre's face. "Well then, she'll be fine there. And I'm not moving if that's what you're insinuating."

"Very well, Missus." Joshua straightens his back as much as his stiff frame allows then backs away still holding her gaze.

Deirdre turns back to my gravesite and asks, "And what do you think?"

She's still standing there waiting for my answer when Reinhart returns with the fire bricks. She walks down to the truck and without looking at him points to a second mound about twenty yards from mine. "Let's put the kiln over there," she says.

"Are you sure, Deirdre?" Reinhart asks, removing his dust-ridden straw hat and running his fingers through a mass of sun-bleached hair. He eyes the hill with a distasteful look. "There may be bones in there, too."

Deirdre looks at him sharply. "You can go easy with the back-hoe, can't you? And if you find anything, stop."

The cords in Reinhart's neck tighten. "The shovel isn't sensitive to such things, Deirdre. And I do have to pick up a certain amount."

He looks at the disappointment mounting on her face and her right shoulder sagging further than usual. Then, he glances at her hands moving toward each other, nails ready to begin scratching.

He takes her hands in his and holds them still. "If you keep doing this Deirdre, you'll get open sores and won't be able to work," he says. "It's only four months since Jacques died. You're expecting too much of yourself. Maybe you've taken on too much moving out here."

Deirdre looks off toward the lake. She can't explain, even to herself, why she spent her last dollar from the sale of her previous home to buy this property.

Reinhart gently shakes her hands to recapture her attention. He turns them over and asks, "Do you have some ointment for these?"

She nods, pulls her hands out of his and gets up. At the screen door, she stops and says, "Please continue with the work, Reinhart."

In the house, she tears off a piece of an aloe vera plant, squeezes the liquid into the palm of her right hand and works it in. She sits down and weeps into the treated hands. Salt works its way into the cracks and stings. She welcomes the feeling.

I feel sorry for her. I wonder if calling on a few souls who have reached a higher level than Jacques would help, perhaps the gentle souls of my ancestors.

The opportunity arises in the evening when she sinks into her porch chair as if all the energy in her has drained straight through her feet. I let her relax and close her eyes. When her mind begins to float, I call on my mother and grandmother to sit with her. Oddly, there's a third one with them, someone I don't recognize. They all perch on the railing. I ask them to be quiet and not scare her. In spite of it, she jolts forward. Her eyelids shoot open. She scoots into the house and drags the bureaus to the doors.

In the morning, when Reinhart arrives, she goes out onto the porch and touches the railing. "Did you notice anyone sitting here yesterday?" she asks.

He shakes his head.

"I'd swear I saw three people." She stares at the railing for several minutes. Then, she abruptly turns to Reinhart and asks, "Do you think I'm here because of good luck or bad luck?" Before he can answer, she adds, "*Baba* used to say land spoke to her. If it told her to settle on it, she did. If it warned her against it, she listened. I thought this land was telling me something positive, but now I'm not so sure."

"I think those bones have rattled you, "Reinhart says, trying to avoid the chuckle rising in his throat. It comes out anyway.

Deirdre casts such a sharp glance at him that he backs off the porch and heads to the kiln site. She sits down in the wooden chair and glances at the pail of clay still sitting by her chair.

I see my chance and forget that I wanted to reassure her about her choice of land. "Pick some up," I say. I repeat it over and over. She finally gets the message, picks up the pail and dumps it on the table Reinhart had placed a sheet of canvas on. She separates a small portion of it and kneads it to remove the air bubbles. She calls it wedging, but to me it looks like kneading a loaf of bread. When she forms a ball with it, she turns it round and round in her hands. "Don't look at the clay," I say. She closes her eyes and holds the ball without moving for a long while. Finally, her fingers begin to move over it. "Yes," I say, "keep going." She smoothes the top and slides her fingers down a bit to form an indentation a quarter of the way down. Below that, she indents again and moves down to form a protrusion. At the bottom, she forms a slight jut out and works her way behind it pinching bits off until about a quarter of the clay has been removed. She picks up a knife, carefully cuts the object in half, straight through the indented and protruding areas, and scoops out the clay from both sides. When finished, she has two shells which she makes little saw-like cuts into along the edges. Then, she bores a hole into the upper indentation on either side, hollows out the second ones and cuts what look like teeth into the lower protrusion on both sides. To complete the structure, she smears a liquid solution of clay and water on the saw-toothed edges and ever so carefully fits the two shells back together and pinches and smoothes the seams.

When she removes her hands, I realize she has sculpted a likeness of my skull. There I am in all my bony glory, only in miniature, and I hadn't even thought of putting that idea into the deepest part of her mind.

Deirdre stands back to look at her creation and straightens with a start. She picks it up and looks as if she's going to throw it back into the pail. A yelp from my back yard stops her. She places the sculpture on a bench against the porch wall and runs down the steps to investigate. Reinhart is jumping around like a jack rabbit, holding his hand.

Talk about luck! Reinhart has gone and smashed his hand unloading the bricks. That should stop him from working. Of course, I hope he's only injured enough to keep him home for a few days. I can't work with all this male energy around. I'll have to be a bit patient, though. Reinhart's hand needs attending to. It's a bloody mess.

Deirdre's a rather good nurse, wrapping Reinhart's hand in a pillow case and loading him into her jeep to cart him off to the hospital. She seems to have lost herself in the emergency. That's the kind of concentration she needs. Twice in one morning! Not bad, Kala, not bad. Kala! Ye gods, I'm becoming the person this woman has imagined.

Hours pass before Deirdre returns. She comes out back and sits on the rock we'd shared just after I'd been dug up. I guess they didn't put the rock back into the hill because it would have disturbed my bones. They've managed to smooth the hill enough without missing it. She looks straight at my place of repose and begins talking: "Kala, I've been thinking. You have shown up when I most need somebody." She gazes into the star-filled sky as if she's looking for someone, or something. "Jacques will never forgive me," she says, turning her eyes back to my grave. "I'll never forgive myself." She's quiet, unusual for her. Until now, she's been dragging out mementoes of Jacques, placing them in the middle of the yard and screaming for his forgiveness.

She pulls up her legs, wraps her arms around them and says, "Kala, I'm so alone. I have a feeling you were alone, too, for your pregnancy. And that your heart ached like mine does."

She's right. Nicholas died of consumption. I know all about guilt. I didn't call Dr. Scott in early enough. And the hospital just up the hill from us. I might have been able to save him. Of course, I eventually rationalized it. The flu epidemic was on its way and, with him so weak, he'd never have survived it. Now that I think of it, a lot of grief has been suffered on this property.

Deirdre, unable to glean any answers from me, or the wind which picks up some of the loose dust on my grave, turns to the business side of things. "Reinhart won't be working for a few days," she says.

Good, I say to myself. Hey, don't blame me for the accident. I had nothing to do with it. Sometimes things happen for a reason. I give him credit for respecting my bones, but I can see he has to have everything scientifically explained.

I summon up Deirdre's grandmother and ask her to sit down beside Deirdre. She reaches out for Deirdre's hand. Deirdre moves her hand to the left, and then pulls it back wondering why she did that. I will her to close her eyes and remain still for several minutes. It takes that long to clear one's mind so its depth can be reached. When she reaches it, she sees her great grandmother dressed in the Ukrainian clothes she always wore on special occasions, a white blouse with criss-cross embroidery and a full skirt, bright crimson, with ribbons flowing from the waist. She has a wreath of wild pink roses on her head. She's not an old woman as Deirdre last saw her, but a woman of forty-five, strong and vibrant. Her arms are outstretched and in her hands is a skull with her name, Kalynka, written on the forehead.

Deirdre's eyes snap open.

Oh dear, maybe I went too far.

I try to will her eyes closed again, but she gets up and runs to the porch. She digs into the pail of clay and works feverishly producing another likeness of a skull. This time, it isn't shaped like me, but like the skull in her mind. Again, she reaches forward looking as if she aims to destroy it. "Leave it alone," I whisper. She obeys and enters the house to wash up. She drops onto her bed and falls asleep immediately.

I rest, too.

We both awaken to a light hammering sound. I know what it is, but Deirdre doesn't. She eases off the bed, shoves her feet into slippers and goes to the window facing my back yard. She sees five people sitting in front of my hill, one tapping a drum and the others chanting. She grabs a poker and runs to the back door. As she opens it, she bumps into Reinhart and almost clobbers him. "Reinhart, I thought you'd be laid up longer than this," she says, lowering the poker.

"I had a hunch you might need me today," he says, swinging his bandaged hand, thumb out, toward the back yard gathering. "I guess we males have a little of that intuition you females talk about." He takes the poker from her and slips his hand beneath her elbow to steer her back into the house. "Let's sit this out a while," he says. "I'll make coffee."

"I'll tell them to leave," Deirdre says.

"Leave them alone. They probably just want to say a few prayers for their dead. Is that old guy who scared you out there?"

Deirdre peers out the kitchen window and looks at each person, finally singling out Joshua. His back is turned towards her, but she recognizes the black hat trimmed with a multi-coloured band that he'd been wearing the day before. She'd thought him to be South American when she first saw him.

"He's there," she says. "He's the drummer. What are we going to do?"

"Just sit quiet, I think."

Deirdre accepts a cup of coffee and stands in front of the window. She has a bewildered look on her face. I can tell she's wondering again what she's done to create such havoc when all she'd wanted was a place in the countryside where she could yell herself through the grief and guilt without disturbing anyone. And hopefully find her creative spirit again.

When the Indians finish chanting, all but one leaves. He pounds stakes around my grave and strings rope on them. I suppose it's being done to mark the area. It certainly won't keep anybody or anything out. I'm getting more attention now than when I died. My father and mother were all that were left, and they were too weak and befuddled to pray.

This drumming was good. My dry old bones came to life a little. I'd like to have danced a bit. I used to love dancing at weddings. The father of the bride would build a platform outside and hire all the district musicians to play two-steps, waltzes and polkas. That's how I met Nicholas. He was a fiddler who played at all the weddings. I danced past him and couldn't help but be charmed. He had a smile as wide as a river and eyes which shone with passion. You could see this was what he was born to do. He brought something out in me I'd never felt before. It was like a gush of water in a freshly dug well. Later, I asked my father to speak to his parents to match him up with me.

I look at Deirdre and Reinhart standing at the window watching this dark brown man close me in and I realize what a fine couple they'd make, both with similar interests – art and nature – and both wounded and in need of human comfort.

Reinhart glances at Deirdre. I detect something in it, perhaps a yearning, but it doesn't last long. He sticks to the matter at hand. "I'm afraid they always fence graves off at excavated areas," he says.

"Will we be able to continue with the kiln?" Deirdre asks. "When your hand is better, I mean."

"I don't know," he answers. "Take a look at this." He reaches into his work shirt pocket and removes a small white object. He hands it to Deirdre.

"What's this?" she asks.

"It's a bone fragment, probably from a child. I found it in the second mound. I think we're due to have these bones assessed, Deirdre."

"Let's do this one and leave Kala alone."

"Okay," Reinhart says, getting up to leave. He hesitates at the door. "I'm just taking it to the museum in Prince Albert. They'll send it on to Regina. How about coming with me? It would do you good to get away for a few hours."

Deirdre shakes her head. "I can't be protected all the time, can I?"

Reinhart checks for Joshua's whereabouts and sees that he's boarding his canoe. He nods and says, "I guess you'll be all right."

After everyone has gone, Deirdre ventures out to my grave, stepping over the rope to reach me. She sinks to the ground and points to the rope. "Kala," she says, "is this what you want?" She looks into the horizon for a long while. Finally, she looks back at my mound and asks, "What happens to you when you die?" She waits a few moments then spills out all the questions which have been on her mind: "Are you safe? Is Jacques safe? Is he happier now? Did you have a husband, Kala? Or did some young brave take advantage of you? Oh, I know, you can't answer me." She looks into the distance again. "When Jacques died, I could tell when his soul departed," she continues. "His face emptied. I didn't know if the soul theory was correct, but at that moment I thought it possible. It's comforting to know something is left of a person when they die. I miss him so, Kala. What am I to do? I didn't mean to hurt him."

She feels a movement inside her abdomen and flicks her hands at it. "And what am I to do with this?" she asks. "I can hardly feed myself. And how am I going to love it while I loathe myself for letting this pregnancy happen?"

I watch another tiny flutter develop in her abdomen and say, "Put your hands on your belly."

She's reluctant until she sees a tiny bump appear. She traces around it with her index finger and says, "I think it's a foot, Kala." I enter her mind to see what she's seeing. She sees the foot, toes fully formed, and allows the image to develop into a full body although she's not sure how developed the fetus is because she hasn't yet seen a doctor. It moves again, this time a shift rather than a jab. She imagines the baby born and holding it at her breast to suckle. A look of pleasure spreads over her face, but it doesn't last long. Another look, a reminder of what she'd like to forget, takes over. She says, "I was weak, Kala." She circles her abdomen. "This child won't even know who its father is. I can't tell him. He has a wife and family." She slumps over in a fit of tears. The tears fall on to my grave. I wish I could do something to help her.

All I can hope for is a few more guides to help her get through this. Sending her great grandmother as a young woman was good. Perhaps youth is better than elders. Maybe more of her relatives. I call on a few. Several men turn up. They walk into the yard and stand beside her. She doesn't respond until a group of women wearing *babushkas* appear on top of the hill holding balls of clay next to their chests. She recognizes them. "Aunt Tina," she says, pointing to the first one. "Aunt Mary. And cousin Petra." As she continues the naming, I take a closer look at the group and notice the spirit, who'd accompanied my mother and grandmother on the railing, marching down the hill.

Who is she? Deirdre doesn't seem to notice anything odd, and I miss hearing the name in my distraction. The women part and let her pass. Then, they all walk down the hill and disappear.

Deirdre stands there bewildered. "Where did they come from?" she asks. "I feel as if I've been transported home and back again." She stands up and faces the wind coming from the north. "But where's home?" she asks. "Kala, where is home?"

"In your clay, Deirdre," I answer. "In your clay." She looks over to the porch and sees that Reinhart has left another covered bucket of clay. She rushes over to remove the plastic and discovers he has worked it up into several balls and left a note telling her he'd tested the clay for cracks and washed out the alkali. She breathes a thank you, picks up one of the balls, flattens it on the table, then picks up another ball and pokes a hole in the middle. She pinches the sides with her thumbs and index fingers. As she pinches, she continuously turns the clay so as to work evenly. It's the basic method for bowl-making. When finished, she sets it aside and removes two more balls from the pail. She flattens one and leaves it on the table while she separates the second one into several pieces. She rolls one of the pieces into a long, rounded strip, coils it, seals the ends together with a thin solution of clay and water and places it on top of the slab. She repeats the process with all the pieces making each one shorter than the last. At the top, she smoothes it closed, rather than leaving it open the way you would for a bowl. She then picks up a knife and cuts several openings into the shape. When she stands back to look at it, she realizes she's done it again – made a skull. She sets it aside to dry and reaches into the pail for more clay. Each construction becomes another skull, all unique in shape and angle. And all miniature. When she has completed eight of them, she stands them on the bench beside the first two, goes inside the house and collapses on her bed.

This does not bode well. She sleeps fitfully, feet constantly jerking. She's also very cold, pulling up an extra blanket to keep warm. I'm thankful when Reinhart returns. He calls her from the truck to let her know it's him. She doesn't answer, so he rushes up the porch steps hoping she hasn't blockaded the door. She hasn't, fatigue having gotten the best of her. He enters and shakes her. She doesn't wake up. He pulls back the blankets to lift her up and finds her lying in a pool of blood. He tries to decide whether to call an ambulance or cut out some time by taking her to the hospital himself. There's little traffic on the road so he can drive fast. He decides to pick her up and take her himself.

At the hospital he's told that she has miscarried. "I'm so sorry," the doctor says. "She looks exhausted. Has she been working too hard or under a lot of stress?" Reinhart nods. The doctor casts him a look which says *you should be ashamed.* "She'll need a few days of our care," he says. "Perhaps you should bring her a few things that will cheer her up – books, magazines, cards from people she knows. Miscarriages usually cause depression for a while."

I think I'm the one who should be ashamed. I pushed her too hard. Whatever gave me the idea that I knew what was best for her? Now it's all up to Reinhart and what does he know about such things? I don't think he and Cassandra have had, or lost, any children. I'm tempted to tell him to bend down and give her a hug like he's been dying to do for several days now, but obviously I'm not the one to advise right now.

Reinhart looks at Deirdre's huddled figure and takes her hands in his. He sees that the nails have been cut to the quick so that she can't tear at her skin. He also notices how dry her skin is and how split the cuticles are. He decides to bring her a bottle of lotion.

Deirdre moans. "I lost her," she says, "just when I was beginning to want her."

Reinhart squeezes her hands. She opens her eyes and scans his face. She sees a look of relief wash over him and wonders how long she's been sleeping. He informs her: "You've been out all day, Deirdre. I'm so glad you're back with us. I was worried I hadn't gotten you here on time."

"I'm not sure I should have been rescued, Reinhart," she says.

I have to get that thought out of her head. When she closes her eyes and sleeps again, I give her something else to think about, what to do with her child. It works. Upon waking, she asks: "Reinhart, can you do me a favour?" At his nod, she says, "Would you make a little box for my baby? I want her to have a proper burial."

Back at the lake, Reinhart finds a pine plank and cuts out the pieces for a small coffin. He constructs it tongue and groove and sands it smooth. He looks for some stain, finds a mahogany colour and brushes it on. He stands back and looks at it. The thought of drawing something on it comes into my head and before another thought arrives I see him climbing the veranda steps to find one of Deirdre's sculpting tools. He soon discovers the mess: dry chunks of clay, dust, pails of stagnant water and the line-up of tiny skulls on the bench. "Christ," he says. "Jesus Christ! How much more morbid can she get?" He stamps out to the yard to get a garbage can.

When he climbs the steps back up to the porch, ready to scoop the first skull into the can, I will him to look at the first sculpture. He does. I will him to look at each one individually to appreciate their differences. He does that, too, noticing that some seem to light up through the openings, others seem to be smiling, and others look so light they almost lift off the bench. He examines each one again. I whisper the word "magic." He looks away, mumbling, "These last few days are affecting my goddamn mind."

Drat! I goofed again.

Fortunately, he can't keep his eyes off the sculptures. He re-assesses each one. "By god," he says. His eyes swing to the kiln site. He ticks off the work left to do in his mind, estimating a week's work if he hurries.

On his hospital visit the following day, he says, "I'm going to have the kiln up and running in a few days. How long do your sculptures need to dry before we can fire them?"

"What sculptures?" Deirdre asks, her voice weary, but the tiredness around her eyes beginning to lift.

"The skulls, Deirdre, on the porch bench." She looks at him blankly and he realizes she must have been in some kind of trance when she constructed them. He decides to stop at the library on his way home and consult a book on clay sculptures for direction. No way is he going to let this collection go.

He changes the subject: "The bone test arrived today. It's Caucasian, Deirdre. A boy about twelve. He's of ethnic descent, probably Slavic."

That would be my brother, Dimitre. I buried him before I got sick.

Deirdre looks at Reinhart, her brows gathering into a question.

"The little bone I found in the second mound. Remember. It means Kala might not be native and we won't have to put up with any more intrusions. You'll need to give me permission to have one of her bones examined, though."

She nods, but seems to have lost focus. "Did you make the box, Reinhart?" she asks, eyes swinging to the window.

"Yes," he says, following her eyes to the window and into a tree beyond it where a sparrow is wavering on a light branch and shaking a piece of fluff in its beak.

Deirdre tilts her head toward the scene. "Getting ready for the little ones," she says. "Such an optimist. I didn't get that chance." She twists a wad of Kleenex in her hands, but doesn't use it preferring to feel the tears slip down her face and to taste their salt.

Upon her return home, Deirdre chooses a name for her baby – Nadia. It comes from the name Nada, meaning hope. I listen to this naming, marveling at the coincidence; that's what I named my first child. I think of my little girl raised by strangers, her surname lost, and suddenly the image of the unrecognizable spirit, who appeared on the hill and on the railing, enters my thick skull.

Reinhart carves the name in large cursive letters on the coffin. He also carves wild roses, their tendrils winding around the name. Deirdre folds the white shawl her grandmother left her into a triangle, wraps Nadia in it and places her in the tiny coffin. She fits the lid on top, noticing that Reinhart has tied a spray of black-eyed-Susans onto it. She gazes at them and wonders what significance they are to him.

Reinhart intuits her thoughts: "My grandmother used to say that black-eyed-Susans lead one to the light."

"German folklore?" she asks.

"No," he says. "A Grandma Schmidt maxim."

He smiles and Deirdre observes how his eyes, clear as the lake when it's still, light up. She smiles back, her eyes reflecting some of the sparkle she'd had before all these tragedies. It makes me think of the sun's rays tipping the waves on the lake in the early morning. I look at her hands reaching out to pick up the coffin. They no longer appear irritated. And light seems to glance off them, too, as she lowers the coffin to its resting place beside me and my little one.

As the child settles in, I also smile. Not because the child is dead, but because my family has come back to me.

SKY CITY

Weary of this trip into the New Mexican desert and the 367′ climb up to one of its mesas, Leah plunked herself down on the top step and refused to look at the adobe settlement stretched out behind her. "It's just another tourist trap," she mumbled, looking down at her arms, bent around her raised knees, and at her hands, clutching her long denim skirt to her legs. Her fingers were swollen from the heat and the exertion. And her nails, she noticed, had been bitten down to the flesh.

Leah's husband, Ferris, standing on the step below, lifted her up and out of the way of approaching tourists. People milled all around them kicking up sand-coloured dust. When Leah ran her tongue between her lips, she found that the residue gritted like fine sandpaper. Raising her eyes, finally, and taking in the two streets, she realized the entire area possessed the very colour and texture of sandpaper. She wondered what made Ferris and all these people choose such a dull place to tour.

She also wondered why a pregnant woman would be inclined to run her hands over several bricks on a building and finger the crevices between them. When the heavyset tour guide joined the woman and also touched the bricks, Leah inched toward them to eavesdrop. "You must be expecting a girl, Madam," the guide said, "and feeling a connection to the Acoma women." He spoke slowly and as though he had something round in his mouth. "Women own these houses, you know. When they die, they pass them on to the youngest daughters."

The pregnant woman glanced up at the man accompanying her. He placed his right hand on the highest part of her swell. Leah winced and turned away. She slipped past Ferris's reach and walked over to the tour group waiting at the edge of the compound.

The guide joined the group and began his memorized spiel. "Acoma, or Sky City as the sign on the highway reads, was first occupied in 1150 A.D. These adobe buildings are about five hundred years old."

A strong wind suddenly swept through the Pueblo swirling soil into everyone's eyes. Several people turned their backs to it; others protected their eyes with their hands. Leah remained still, eyes unblinking. The guide covered his left ear and hunched into his blue wind breaker, hands tucked into the opposite sleeves. "The early adobes were made of straw and clay," he continued," the later ones of brick. The clay and straw were carried up the steps some of you climbed. The bricks were made at the bottom of the mesa and lifted up by rope."

Ferris gazed at his wife as she allowed the sand to tear her eyes. She was punishing herself again, he knew, for Stacey's fall. He'd so hoped this trip would be the catalyst she needed to take her mind off it and enable her to move on to the mending process the Hospice people spoke about. He'd tried to make her face the house and the yard without Stacey, as they advised, but it hadn't worked. He'd decided, in the end, that Leah needed to experience a landscape that would dry her sorrow. What better contrast to the winter rains of Vancouver than the deserts of New Mexico? As he'd planned the trip, he imagined the desert sun a warm hand, its fingers reaching into Leah's inner core. He wanted the sun to heal that core and give him back the woman he married.

She still looked like that woman, still the large-boned chunky girl with the side-parted brown hair that hung straight and loose to her shoulders. But she no longer carried her body erect or swung her hair back over her left shoulder in that cocky manner to which he'd been so attracted. And the glint of sun in the azure of her eyes was now clouded over. Dull. Much like the cistern water stored in the small pools around this complex.

Leah rubbed her eyes at last and leaned against a building. She quickly straightened, however, and moved away. The bricks on the building were cool. The colour suggested warmth. So did the air.

Things had a way of fooling her. She'd been fooled into thinking Stacey was improving in the hospital – her temperature had gone down and she'd stopped whimpering long enough to fall asleep – and actually allowed herself to be talked into going home to get some sleep herself. She'd never forgive herself for that. Never.

The guide led the group to the edge of the mesa, hands still thrust into his sleeves. "Conquistadors discovered Acoma between 1539 and 1598 when they rode through the opening below us." He leaned over the edge and looked down. Leah grabbed the right sleeve of his jacket and yanked him back. She was relieved that she'd been standing so close to him. If she'd stayed close to Stacey, Stacey would never have reached the monkey bars ahead of her. But Stacey had asked for a purple popsicle so sweetly that Leah had run back into the house, just for the minute it took to pull out the freezer tray and run warm water over it to loosen the popsicle.

The guide removed Leah's hand from his sleeve and circled the group until he was a good distance from her. He resumed his talk: "The conquistadors demanded food, supplies, and labour. Our people finally revolted on December 4, 1598. The skirmish left the Acoma people hesitant to welcome foreigners. This changed only when Father Juan Ramirez rode through the opening later that year and witnessed an Acoma child step over the edge and plunge down."

Leah knelt down and looked over the edge. She reached and pulled back as though pulling someone up. A tall woman in a long beige skirt and blue work shirt tried to coax her away from the cliff. Ferris grabbed her arms from behind, pulled her upright and walked her to the steps of a three-storey building.

"I had her," Leah cried. "She was there. In my arms. I had her. Why didn't you leave me there? I could have saved her. She'd be sitting here with me right now."

Ferris settled her on the bottom step and tried to soothe her. The pregnant woman offered Ferris her canteen. He poured some of the water in his hands and dabbed Leah's face. Leah leaned forward, arms still out in the reaching motion, fingers curved. "I'm so sorry, Stacey," she cried. "I'm so sorry." Then, looking the pregnant woman straight in the eye, she said, "They die anyway." The woman backed away.

It was always the same, Leah trying to bring Stacey back and lashing out at anyone who was vulnerable, and Ferris standing by saying, "You've got to stop torturing yourself, Leah."

When Leah was calm enough to stand up, Ferris took her hand and led her back to the group. The woman in the blue work-shirt smiled at Leah and said, "The story had a good ending, dear. The priest caught the child and returned it to her mother." Leah turned away and walked toward the pottery displays.

Ferris followed her, his slender frame as rigid as the adobe buildings he walked towards. He singled out a potter in front of one of the buildings and stopped before her. He ran his fingers through his thinning hair and adjusted his expression from exasperation to interest. "Good morning, Senorita," he said, his voice so light it even surprised him. "What do you have to show us today?"

The potter opened her arms and fanned her offerings, palms upward, long fingers spread. Her eyes scanned both Ferris and Leah's faces. They settled on Leah's. Leah jammed her hands into her skirt pockets and looked at the ground. She circled the scuffed toe of her brown leather boot in the sand.

The potter picked up a tiny squat vessel with a small hole in the middle and held it out to Leah. Ferris reached in front of Leah and opened his hand to receive it. The vessel was rust-coloured with black turtles painted all around its base. They were in various stances, one with its head cocked to the right, one upside down, feet waving, and two others walking straight ahead. "Turtles bring good luck," the potter said. When she saw the quizzical look on Ferris's brow, she added, "It's a seed pot. You place seeds inside and sprinkle them into the soil."

"How do you get the seeds inside?" he asked.

Leah glanced back at the tour group which was ascending the hill to the church Father Ramirez was famous for building. It was a block-shaped building with towers on either side. She noticed a child squatting in the sand beside the church. That's what Stacey had been doing by the monkey bars in their yard when Leah ran in for the popsicle. Squatting and drawing pictures in the dirt with a stick.

She couldn't believe Stacey had scaled the climbing apparatus by herself. She'd always been afraid to. Leah couldn't remember Stacey's fall, just the grape popsicle still in her hand in the ambulance and the purple stains on the sheet which covered Stacey's colourless body.

Leah took a deep breath. She darted her eyes about and let them settle on another Acoma woman across the street. The woman placed her most colourful pots at the front of her table. A child appeared and stood to the left of the woman. She pinched off a piece of dough from a large ball in a metal bowl and began to pat it. She had dark skin and straight black hair which hung in points to her waist. The woman placed a frying pan on the hot plate beside her. She dropped a bit of water into it to check the temperature. The droplets danced, so she poured oil in the pan. She picked up the child's dough, spun it around on her fist, and placed it in the pan. It sizzled, sending wafts of doughy smells into the air. She flipped the flat round bread over and prepared a basket to put it in. All the while she worked, she watched Leah.

Leah's face was broad, like hers, and almost as brown, though it seemed undernourished and lifeless. The woman smiled at Leah and crooked her finger. Leah walked towards her, moving as if a line had been drawn on the ground and she must step one foot in front of the other until she reached the end of it. On arrival, the woman offered Leah the basket of bread. Leah accepted it and tried to smile at the child who was patting another piece of dough. She bit off a piece of the crisp edge. As the saliva mixed with the fresh yeast, an intense hunger overcame her. She took bite after bite while the woman looked on. When finished, she felt foolish that she'd forgotten to pay the woman. She reached into her pocket and pulled out a dollar. With it came the small framed photo of Stacey that she always carried. Before realizing it, she placed it in the woman's hands with the money. The woman looked at the photo for a few moments, and then handed it back to Leah. The frame was hot. Leah dropped it. When she bent to pick it up, the child got there first, snatched it between her thumb and index finger and slipped it in the front pouch of her sweatshirt. Leah reached out to grab the photo, but the child had disappeared. Leah glanced up and down the street for the girl, and up the stairs of a nearby building. She began walking toward the stairs. "Leah," the child's mother called. Leah turned around. "Ana is in there," she said, pointing to a door behind her. Leah returned and walked through the door the woman held open. She wondered how the woman knew her name, but before she could inquire she was inside standing in front of the child. The child sat rocking in a wooden chair. Leah held out her hand and asked for the photo. The child shook her head and held the pouch of her sweatshirt open to show Leah it was empty. Leah glanced at the woman.

"Ana, stop playing games," the woman said. "Go get the picture." Once again, the child vanished.

"She'll give it back to you," the woman said. She beckoned Leah to follow her as she walked through the crowded living, bedroom area at the front of the dwelling to the cluttered kitchen at the back. She bent down to pull out an aluminium pan from under the table and removed two lumps of clay. She handed one of them to Leah. "We might as well do something while we wait for Ana," she said. The woman divided her clay into several portions and began to knead one of them. "Clay must be kneaded like bread," the woman said. As Leah worked the clay in the palms of her hands, she stole glances around the tiny living space wondering where Ana slept. She'd noticed only one bed in the front room.

The woman flattened her clay, set it aside, and picked up a fresh piece. She shaped it into another ball, placed it on the table, and rolled it into a long snakelike strip. Deftly circling the flattened piece with the strip, she sealed the ends and said, "You make several and put one on top of the other."

In tandem, the women rolled, placed, and sealed until two vessels stood in front of them. Leah stepped back and surveyed her creation. She looked up at the finished pottery on the shelf. "How do you shape it to look like those?" she asked. It seemed incredible that anything so beautiful could spring from such a crude beginning. The completed pieces were smooth and painted white. The foregrounds of each piece sported various kinds of rust-coloured birds and black animals surrounded by borders of flowering plants and geometric patterns of black, white and rust.

The woman picked up two flat, sharp objects. She handed one to Leah and began smoothing out the coil ridges on the outside of her pot with the other one. She supported it from the inside with her free hand.

"What is this?" Leah asked, holding the object up to the window light.

"A piece of gourd," the woman answered.

Leah scraped the clay. "Can this pottery actually be used?" she asked. She glanced out of the window behind the woman. Perhaps Ana had slipped outside.

"Oh, yes," the woman said. "For cooking. For carrying." She formed a mouth on her vessel by squeezing the clay between her thumb and forefinger.

Leah picked up a finished bowl, looked inside, and ran her fingers over it. She slipped one finger inside the lip and placed her thumb on the outside. "But, it's so thin," she said, pulling her hand back. "It feels brittle." It reminded her of how delicate Stacey had been when she was born. At first, she'd called her mother to help her change and bathe Stacey. Stacey's arms and legs looked so fragile she was afraid she'd break them.

"It feels and looks delicate," the woman said, "but we put potsherds in the clay to make it strong."

"Potsherds?"

"Ground up pieces of old pottery. I also use rainwater to prepare the clay." Leah raised her eyebrows. "Rain water is free of hard elements, like iron. Hard elements can dissolve in the clay and make it weak." The woman's dark aqueous eyes searched Leah's face. They fixed upon her eyes.

Leah felt as if she were standing in two pools of water too deep to climb out of. She attempted to look away, but couldn't. She tried to blink. Her eyelids wouldn't budge. She willed her fingers to flex, and when they obeyed, directed them to the top of her pot. The movement broke the eye contact. Unnerved, Leah decided to quickly finish her pot and get out of the house.

Her hands, though, seemed apart from her mind. They began moving at a snail's pace. Reaching out. Picking up the pot. Turning it around and around to display the imperfections. Then, putting it back on the table. The palms of her hands smoothed the pot inch by inch. The fingers indented the top and formed the mouth.

"This is as much as we can do today," Leah heard the woman say. "The pots must dry now." She sounded as though she were speaking from the opposite side of the mesa. Leah looked up to see if the woman was still there. She was, but her body seemed undefined. Leah's hands reached for the pot and held it out to the woman. As it left her hands, the woman's body resumed its shape and walked over to a cupboard on which a clay basin stood. She reached up to a shelf, pulled down a gourd, and poured water into the basin. Every inch of the woman's body seemed over-defined now: the large hands with grey clay permanently imbedded under the fingernails, the plaited black hair half way down her back, the thick waist still apron-wrapped, and the round, pleasant face etched too early by the sun.

"We use rain water and it doesn't rain much here," she said, as an apology for pouring so little water into the basin. She motioned Leah to wash first. Reluctantly, Leah placed her hands into the basin. She had liked the feeling of the clay on her fingers, pulling the skin taut against the bones. Instead of washing, she wanted to go outside and let the sun, which was now shining hotly on the mesa, dry the clay on her hands. She wanted the clay to crack and fall off. She wanted the skin and flesh to fall too, leaving her bones exposed until they became dry and white. She wished someone would spread clay over her entire body and lead her into the sun to dry.

As Leah dried her hands, she felt something pulling on her skirt. She looked down hoping to see Ana at her feet. She wasn't there. Leah moved away from the wash stand to make room for the woman. "Do you think Ana will want to learn how to make pottery?" she asked.

"Ana knows everything now," the woman said. She turned from the basin and smiled. She tried to look into Leah's eyes once again. Leah fastened her eyes on the pot she'd shaped.

The woman dried her hands and placed the towel on a hook above the stand. "Would you like to take the pot home?" she asked. Leah nodded. The woman pointed at a square box in the corner of the room. Leah picked it up and set it on the table. The woman gently transferred the pot into the box and taped the top. "You can come back in a few days and I'll show you how to finish it," she said, placing her hand on Leah's back and leading her out of the dwelling.

Outside, she was hustled off by Ferris who also placed his hand on her back. "I've been going half-crazy looking for you," he said.

"My photo," Leah said. "I have to get my photo." Ferris led her up the hill to the church without responding. She said it again and looked up at him. Still no response. In front of the church, Leah asked Ferris if he'd bought the seed pot. He nodded and patted the bag he wore slung over his shoulder. Leah breathed a sigh of relief. *I must not have said it loud enough*, she thought.

On the hill, the guide was droning on. "This is the graveyard," he said, pointing to a fenced off area. "There are three layers of graves here." He sliced the air laterally with a flat hand. "Dirt to build it up has been brought up in buckets from the bottom of the mesa." Leah looked at the dun-coloured earth dotted with brightly coloured artificial flowers and drew the pottery box close to her bosom. Panic began to rise from the pit of her stomach. Stacey was lying in a graveyard at home, thousands of miles away. Alone. Her eyes glazed over. Ferris reached out to relieve her of the box so that he could hold her hand until the spell passed. Leah dug her fingers into the cardboard and backed away from him.

"I'm sorry, Leah," he said, hands falling listlessly to his sides. "I didn't know this was here."

Leah took several gulps of air. She angled her body toward the church and without looking at Ferris, said, "Why don't you stay with the group? I'm going into the church and I don't need you with me." Her voice sounded cold and separate from her.

She pivoted and walked inside. As she dipped her fingers in the holy water at the back of the church, her strength ebbed. She was tempted to sit down on the cool tiles rather than make her way all the way to the front where a few pews sprawled to the left and right. Her feet, however, shuffled forward. She sat down in the front pew on the right and glanced around the altar area. It was meagre, just high white walls and a painting of the patron saint, St Estephan del Rey. She looked up at the nondescript white ceiling, then down into a pair of large brown eyes. It was the child – no more than a foot away from her. The arc of the child's mouth curved into the same shape as her eyebrows.

"You're lucky today, Leah," she said. Her eyes exuded the smile her lips avoided.

"How am I lucky?" Leah asked, moving over to make room for the child to sit down. "You haven't even given back the picture of my little girl. That doesn't seem lucky to me."

"Did you hear the wind outside?" the child asked. She cupped her hand over her left ear.

"No," Leah admitted.

"There are voices in it. They are the Pueblo's spirits. All the Pueblo's spirits stay in the city and visit us. Sometimes they get together in this church. On those days, no one can open the doors. You're lucky today because the doors are open."

"What difference would open doors make to spirits?" Leah asked.

"None," said the child. "But spirits that have not been let free need open doors."

The child pulled a candle and a pack of matches out of her sweatshirt pouch. She placed the matches on top of the pottery box Leah still held in her arms. Leah put the box on the bench, picked up the matches and struck one. She lit the candle and took it from Ana. The flame flickered, and then burnt straight up. Leah's head felt airy. Her body swayed. She held her hand out to Ana for support. Ana placed her hand firmly in Leah's. After a few moments, she lifted Leah's arm as high as her own arm would extend, and let her hand drift away from Leah's. Leah stared at their hands suspended in the air. Their fingers seemed transparent. Her vision blurred for a moment. She blinked to clear it. When she lifted her eyelids, Ana was no longer there.

The candle flickered and cast its shadow over the box on the bench. A sudden urge to open the box overcame Leah. She reached for it and peeled off the tape. She looked inside and, to her surprise, discovered the pot was gone. But the photo of Stacey was there, smiling even more brilliantly than Leah remembered. She lifted the photo out of the box. As she nestled it in her hands, the heavy doors of the church swung shut.

THE HARROW MAN

Vern Halliday didn't see the woman until his harrow almost touched her bare outstretched foot. She wasn't supposed to still be on the beach. She always walked off when she saw him coming.

"I'm sorry," he said to her out of his truck window. "I didn't see you there." She was sitting beneath a poplar tree which was shedding its spring catkins. He glanced at the mounds of white debris forming under the tree and wondered how he'd pick it all up.

The woman closed her notebook and pulled in her legs. She tucked the book into a grey carryall while Vern sat waiting. He removed his cap and ran his fingers over his freshly shaved head. He wasn't yet accustomed to bareness. He twisted the cap in his hand and traced around its inscription, "Vern's Landscaping," with his index finger.

As the woman got up, he noticed she wore her usual grey clothing: leggings, scooped neck shirt, and long vest. Her hair, a mass of two-toned grey, hung over her face. When she lifted her head to look up at him, he drew back in surprise. Her skin, ripple-free and translucent, defied her hair.

"I'm sorry," he said again, his brows gathering into inverted V's. The woman got up and backed away.

Vern checked his side mirror, then the rear-view mirror. He caught a glimpse of himself and cringed. No wonder she's backing away, he thought. I look like a god damn criminal. He jammed the cap back onto his head and brought the peak down low. He had shaved his head to keep himself from banging it on the edge of his bathroom sink.

He had been up all night with David, the youngest of his three boys, holding his lurching body over the toilet bowl. David was bedded down now, in the narrow back seat of his truck because his sitter, wouldn't you know, had called in sick herself. He'd tried to get his wife up to fill in for the sitter while doling out Cheerios for the twins, Benjamin and Jonathon. "Misty," he'd called from the kitchen. "Misty, I need you this morning."

She'd groaned. "No, I can't."

"Misty, I mean it. Misty." He'd stood at the door, pouring milk into one of the cereal bowls.

"Christ," she'd said, picking up a glass half full of gin and throwing it at him.

She'd turned over and promptly begun to snore. He'd felt so frustrated he'd wanted to bang his head on the door frame. David's tired whine from his bedroom brought him back to his senses. But when he'd begun shaving, he'd looked down to the edge of the sink and wondered what a head meeting porcelain would feel like.

Before the shaving, his hair was black and thick. "Like thatch," Misty used to say. That was in their early days when they bathed together and she would lather it generously. "You could have lumps all over your head and no one would ever notice," she would say, laughing. He remembered her small breasts pressed against his back. She always hugged him when she laughed.

He ground the gearshift into first while watching the woman leave the beach. Her steps were graceful, he noticed, and her swing loose. He thought of her grey eyes, clear and still, like the lake water on calm mornings. He mouthed the word "sorry" again, realizing he wasn't as sorry for the dust his harrow would create as he was about her leaving. Over the month he had been arriving early to gaze at her cascade of grey hair falling over a notebook, he had begun to think of her as something mystical - perhaps something risen from the lake.

She seemed akin to the birds and could sit still for long periods of time to watch them. She often singled out one bird to study. Occasionally, he tried to watch one of her studies but could never figure out what was so fascinating about it. It was just a bird doing bird things, as he was just a man doing man things.

Man things. Driving a truck. Picking up garbage. Tidying up the beach for people to come and mess up again. The only footprints he could tolerate in his harrowed sand were the woman's, but she always got up and left when she saw him coming.

He knew she timed herself by him. She would be home by 8 a.m., doing whatever a woman like that did.

Now that he had seen her face, he wanted her to live alone up there on the mountain she always headed toward. He imagined her making breakfast, cutting up fruit, perhaps toasting a croissant or a bagel. She would take the food out to her garden and sit there by a pond, contemplating what to do later on. She wouldn't have coffee since she'd already had some on the beach. Each morning as she left, he saw her toss a paper cup into the garbage can.

He visualized the pond: tiered rocks with water cascading, yellow water lilies floating above a family of orange koi fish, and reeds swaying along the eastern edge. He saw the fish nudging the edges for food and the woman complying, the double wooden swing still swaying behind her. He figured her to be creative: a writer, a painter, or perhaps a potter. He hadn't seen her hands, though. He didn't know if she had a callous on the inside of her middle finger, paint in the creases of her skin, or clay beneath her nails.

He glanced down at his own hands, big clumsy things clutching the steering wheel, and thought about how agile they once were. How he could sweep a landscape with his out-turned palm, or curve his forefinger into his thumb to allow a peephole no bigger than a camera lens. He had loved the large and the small of everything around him. Those were the days he could have boasted a name like "Keshiki Gardens" or something with "Landscape Design" in it. He was very good at surveying the environment and graphing out what would suit the lay of the land, his specialty having been small Japanese gardens. He looked at the whole picture back then.

Then, Misty had fit right into the picture - the Misty he liked to remember. The woman he once compared to the soft mist that often slipped into the valley on October mornings and wound its arms around the mountains, trees, and domestic landscapes. He shook his head to clear this image, but wished he hadn't, because a more recent one surfaced - the Misty who began her day in the wisps of yesterday's alcohol, worked her way into a thick net by afternoon, and lost sight of herself by evening.

He revved the truck motor to sound like he was resuming work, while taking a last look at the woman as she slipped into her loafers and crossed the highway. Finally, he released the clutch and pressed on the gas pedal. As he drove back and forth, he wondered what the woman had been writing. More specifically, he wondered if the notebook was a diary. It was larger than a diary, though, and coiled. Not the little ruled "Day by Day" book he'd seen his sister, Belinda, write in when he was a child, and which he tried to steal because she taunted him. "You get everyone to think you're such a hotshot with those fancy gardens you draw," she once said. "But I see you crying in your little hiding place. You're just a baby, Vern, crying when you don't get what you want. And I know how many times because it says so right here in my diary."

He *had* cried. He'd cried for the return of his mother, that tall willow of a woman who cuddled him and told him, "I'm so happy you were born." She was an artist. He remembered accompanying her whenever she installed sculptures. Her works of art were huge and stood before him like dark phantoms. When he was a toddler they frightened him. Later, he thought of them as story characters, such as the ones his mother showed him in Greek and Roman art books. "Look at this Chimera," she'd say. "It has three animals in it." She'd take the index finger of his left hand and trace around the heads of a lion, snake, and goat. "Here's Bellerophon trying to overtake it on his horse," she'd say. "He was very special because he tamed Pegasus with a magic bridle and rode him to Mount Olympus." He'd beg her to find the Pegasus story and show him where Mount Olympus was on the map. She'd become so excited a bit of spittle would form in the corner of her mouth.

Vern particularly liked the she-wolf who suckled Romulus and Remus. He liked it because his mother used the word "suckled" instead of fed and because the twins appealed to him. He'd often thought of being a twin himself and having an amiable brother instead of a smart aleck sister. He imagined himself and his brother, Victor, curled up on their mother's lap, mouths open to suckle whatever she offered, be it milk or words or just a warm smile. Because he was so young at the time, his mother hadn't told him of the demise of Remus. As an adult, Vern realized that he, like Romulus, had to kill his own twin, in order to present himself as an individual in a society lacking duality.

"Someday I'm going to visit the real she-wolf in Rome," he would say to his mother when she closed the book and returned it to the shelf. To partially satisfy his desire for the real thing, she took him to galleries and lifted him up to touch the flanks of a goat or dog, the span of a snake's body or an eagle's wing, and the furrows in a woman's robe and a man's brow.

Yes, he had cried for his mother, because he could remember the pictures and sculptures more vividly than he remembered her. Her face had faded a little more each day until it was only a smear in his memory, like a photo taken from a fast-moving train.

He'd also cried for the subsequent loss of his mother's friend, Mineko, a Japanese woman who sculpted bonsai trees with just the right pinches and planted cherry trees, lilies, and chrysanthemums to keep them company. She worked with his mother on park projects. He had been allowed to plant alongside Mineko when his mother's Zen arches and bridges were given homes. As they scooped dirt and planted, she told him about the god Inari. "He comes down from the mountains in the springtime to guide the rice planting and to assure riches for the farmers." She talked about the sculpture she'd seen of Inari and his two messenger foxes when she had been so fortunate to visit her sister in Japan. "It is a masterpiece, little Vernon," she said. She also talked about the Japanese tranquility she experienced while there. "Child," she said, "there is too much chaos in this world."

Mineko's face wasn't clear anymore either, but he remembered her hair. It was long and grey and she didn't pull it back. It fell over her face while she worked, just like the beach woman's hair. He imagined the beach woman, finished breakfast now, and moving about her yard with pruning shears in her hands. He concentrated on the hands, thinking of the tales cuticles and lines could tell and how attitude could be revealed through gesture. He must try to see the beach woman's hands next time he's close enough. Mineko's fingers were long and, he supposed, beautiful at one time, but the knuckles had thickened with manual work and the cuticles were ragged. It was the grace of them, though. How they floated from basket to earth. How they transferred love to his face with the slightest touch.

He thought about the notebook in the beach woman's hands. How she snapped it closed whenever he came close to her. A niggling fear made its way up his spine. Perhaps the beach woman was writing about him. Perhaps she'd seen him lurking behind the canoe building. Perhaps she would report him to the police, leaving him without a reasonable way to explain that he just needed to be near her. Near something she had and he didn't.

He knew the woman's routine. Knew she walked down to the beach and tucked her carryall under the bush alongside the canoe building each morning. Knew she went for a walk down Kalavista Road for at least twenty minutes before settling onto Kal beach. One day, when she was a safe distance away, he snatched up her bag from its hiding place and removed the notebook. He sat down in the brush and flipped through the pages, then flipped through them again. To his dismay, there wasn't one written word in it, not even her name. The book was a sketchpad filled with quick drawings of birds in every stance possible. Grebes with uplifted beaks. Gulls standing on one leg. Geese skittering on the lake water, wings prepared for flight. One sketch in particular caught his attention - a heron's beak in a shaft of light. No body, just a long, slender, white beak. The shaft of light resembled a spike piercing the water. It looked like it had been pounded right into the floor of the lake. As he stared at the image, the sensation of being pinned down himself passed through him, and then vanished. He closed the book and mourned having to return it to the carryall under the bush.

That afternoon, he found Misty sitting up in bed, sorting photographs. He brought her a snack on a tray and sat down beside her. She waved the snack away and lit a cigarette. A full glass of gin teetered on the bed stand. He pushed it back and for just a moment allowed his recurrent wish to surface, the one in which Misty drops her cigarette on the bed and burns the entire house down, her included. It was a nasty desire, but he couldn't think of any other way out. He'd already tried the hospital clinics a half dozen times, but she always kicked and screamed and swore at him, accusing him of abandoning her. He'd finally realized it was he who wanted her cured, not Misty herself.

Secretly, he accused his sister, Belinda. She was the one who invited Misty to her hideaway in the mountains. She was the one who plied her with liquor. And where was that god-damn Belinda now?

He looked down at Misty, who was trying to place two photos on the sticky peeled back page of the album. Her hands shook so much she kept getting the photos crooked. He took the photos from her and arranged them. A bit of sun spilled in through the half-open blind and highlighted one of the pictures. It was of Misty and his sister. They stood ankle deep in water, holding hands and smiling at each other. He avoided looking at Misty's image - her golden hair lifting in the breeze, her eyes reflecting the cerulean water, her body appearing light enough to fly - and glanced instead at the face of his sister, Belinda. He picked up the album and brought it closer to his eyes. Here was a face he didn't know anymore, a face that used to appear tight and taunting to him, and which now portrayed ease and kindness. He saw something else, too – love and commitment. Unable to deal with the truth on that face, he glanced at the background, a flock of geese flying in formation, pinning an early moon to the blue, blue sky.

*

As the summer waned, Vern found himself spending more and more time watching what the beach woman gazed at, trying to figure out what she would catch at the end of her pastel crayons. One day, she seemed to be looking far up the lake. He grabbed the binoculars he had found on the beach the previous day and brought the lake up close. Two white-throated grebes swam, yellow bills bent for the kill of small fish. She couldn't possibly see those bills, though. It had to be the glide she was watching; the grace of their necks. He liked that. He also liked the idea of being able to see something she couldn't.

Another time, she seemed to be staring right through a gathering of seagulls. He finally located the bird capturing her attention, a grey seagull grasping a flip-up carton in its beak. It resembled a beggar walking about with an alms box. As he watched the gull stagger under the weight of the box, he saw the gestures of Misty in it, the way she reached for him, begging him to understand, telling him, "I'll try to stop. Yes, I'll try. I'll do it tomorrow. I will, Vern, truly."

It was clear the woman on the beach didn't drink. Not a trace of broken blood vessels on her skin. Eyes bright. Cheeks pink from the fresh air and slight breeze wafting over the lake. The leaves above her moved gently, as did her hair. It surprised him that he'd noticed all that the morning he came so close to her with the harrow. He even recalled her bare feet, so vulnerable. He imagined them webbed.

This took him straight back to eight years old and the voice of his father reading him "I Wish that I had Duck Feet" by Theo. Lesieg. He so loved the power the boy character fathomed up by wearing duck feet to face the neighbourhood bully that he eagerly learned to read the book himself. He visualized pulling those webbed feet onto his own feet and wearing the deer horns the protagonist also wanted to wear. And, he imagined stomping into Belinda's room, tying her up with a rope, and hanging her and her blasted diary high up on his horns.

Compared to his thorny sister, Misty had been all smooth bark and fragrant flowers. "You're nothing like Belinda," he recalled telling her.

"I hope not," she said, "after the stories you've told me."

They rented horses, rode bareback, and planned a Zen garden over picnic lunches under wild willow trees. They'd also made what Vern thought was sweet and passionate love under those trees. Family was excluded until plans of marriage developed. When he took Misty to meet his family, he wasn't prepared for the instant attraction and ensuing friendship she and Belinda would develop. In later years, he became jealous. "You spend more time with my sister than me," he often said, his dark face pinched and hurt. "Sometimes I wonder which one of us you love."

He was equally unprepared for the change in Misty after Belinda died of breast cancer. "She was my first female friend," she'd sobbed at the funeral. "I can't live without her." He'd stood by her side, one arm awkwardly wound around her shoulders. That was the last time she let him touch her. The last time he saw her sober. And the last time he felt compelled to design gardens. He poured concrete over the back yard and set up a basketball hoop for the boys. When the front yard became a mass of dandelions, he sprayed them with Round Up and dumped pebbles on it.

*

Toward the end of summer, Vern slowly made his way to the beach hoping the beach woman would be there. When he didn't see her at first, he became unnerved. He was used to routine, liked routine. Didn't know how he would get through a day without sameness. He looked up and down the beach, until he spotted her sitting at the water's edge by the pier. She was sitting beside a map of the world she had drawn in the sand. Two mallards stood plumb in the middle of the map eating bits of the fritter she threw to them. As they became more familiar, they edged closer and closer to snatch the offerings from the palm of her hand. He edged closer, too, until he could hear her saying, "Little birds, this is bad for you." She laughed and took a bite herself. "Bad for all of us," she said, laughing again. It seemed to Vern that the laughter circled around her and the ducks the way concentric circles form around surfacing fish. He thought of how all things circled. The earth. The moon. The sun. Life.

He liked the beach woman scene so much he wished he had brought a camera to capture it. When the sun escaped from a cloud and highlighted the beach woman's hands, he paid close attention, noticing a bit of paint etched into the wrinkles of her knuckles. Her hands were that of an old woman, loose skin covered with brown spots. He glanced up from her hands to her eyes. She nodded and gazed at him, then picked up a poplar twig lying beside her and circled the map in the sand. "There's too much chaos in this world," she said.

*

Later that day, Vern impulsively picked up his children early from school and took them to the beach. He watched the twins jump off the dock and swim beneath it, in and out of the spaces between the supporting poles. And when David finished splashing about in the shallow water, Vern sat near him to demonstrate how ancient people navigated on the sea. "In the old days," he told the boy, "people found their way by watching the stars and drawing maps in the sand." He made X's where he and David were, where the concession stand stood, and where their truck was parked. David added roads to downtown, school, and home. He marked those spots with big X's as well.

As he watched, Vern felt a stream of warmth enter his body and extend itself to the boy. He reached his hand to David's face and neck, and gently traced the contours of them. His own face softened and the pupils in his deep brown eyes narrowed to encircle only his little family. He sat back, bristly head bare to the sun, and idly twisted a stick in the sand. When he looked down, he saw that he'd drawn a house edged by a creek and surrounded by yew trees. It was far away from David's grid. And his X had become a bird, wings outstretched.

THE PACT

Marta's fourteen now and has been demanding I take her to British Columbia to see the house her parents, Vita and Richard, settled her in when they brought her home from Romania. She can only recall bits of it: her crib, the flowers on the walls in her mother's room, soft voices, and light slanting across her mother's face from the big window lined with bars. She now knows the bars are called vertical blinds, but she didn't know that then. Then, they looked like the bars on her crib.

"It's me this time," Vita said, when I arrived at the Vernon Jubilee Hospital in January, 1991. "Before it was them." She named three women – Luella, Bridget and Fiona - punctuating each name with a pencil dot on a notepad in her lap. "Luella's doing everything she did before. And Bridget's hair is coming back in. Sometimes she doesn't even wear the wig she bought. Would you believe she bought a curly wig?"

"Her hair was straight, was it?" I asked, going along with her nervous chatter for the moment.

She nodded and lifted a pair of reading glasses onto her nose, two gold chains trailing. "I'll buy a straight blonde wig," she said, as she printed the word "wig" slowly on the notepad with her left hand.

I looked at her dark, unruly curls and down at her left hand beginning another word, "bra," letters all slanted in the wrong direction. Her right hand dangled from an arm sling.

"Why is your arm in a sling?" I asked.

She added "padded on one side" in parenthesis. "They took some lymph nodes," she said. She bit her lip and wrote two more items: "Metamucil" and "Ensure." Each word was an act of labour requiring the use of the eraser on the end of the pencil.

As I watched her, I remembered how she'd always written lists, even at the age of thirteen when we'd met on the landing leading to our second floor dormitory. She'd stood there staring at the list of things she was supposed to do, tears rolling down her cheeks.

We'd both been dumped in a convent boarding school, she, because she was one too many in a fatherless clan of seven children, and me, because my tyrant father was sick and tired of having his authority challenged. When I saw Vita on the landing crying like that, and learned she'd come on the train by herself and no one had been at the station to meet her, I proclaimed: "To hell with parents and anyone who has anything to do with them," and took her by the arm to climb the rest of the steps.

Now, as she printed and erased, I wondered if lists postponed reality for her or if they were her way of toughening herself up. What would I do in her place? Lists wreaked havoc. Being a journalist, I'd probably record every second of the experience, but I wouldn't make lists.

She added "thank you notes" to her list. "The nurses have been incredible," she said. "And look at all these flowers." She swept her hand around the room. Bright bouquets of roses, carnations, chrysanthemums, astromeria and the odd tropical flower lined the window sill and teetered on the bedside cabinet. I counted eleven in all. Overwhelming in a room already crowded with electronic monitors, an intravenous apparatus and the mandatory furnishings of bed, swing table, cabinet and two gold vinyl armchairs.

"The threat of war in the Gulf certainly hasn't upstaged you," I said, looking straight into her face in an attempt to make her look at me.

She tore off the notebook page, folded it and tucked it under her pillow. She took a deep breath in and blew it out through her mouth. "I'm going to leave the woes of the world to others for a while," she said, finally glancing up at me. "I have to, for Marta."

I saw then how dull her eyes had become and how the skin around them was dark and crinkled. I also noticed how thin her face was. Deep lines had formed alongside her mouth. And her skin was tinged a pale yellow. As a young woman, she'd always had a clear, pink complexion, lively chocolate brown eyes and an impish half-smile on her lips.

I pulled one of the chairs away from the wall, placed it beside Vita's bed and sat down on its edge wondering what to say about Marta. I knew Vita and Richard had adopted a three year old child from an orphanage in Romania two years previously because Vita had sent an announcement card. I had returned a "Congratulations" card, but we hadn't exchanged calls or letters since. I'd been busy running between Toronto and Kosovo and she obviously needed to learn the art of parenting as fast as possible. I didn't even know she'd been battling breast cancer until her Aunt Nora called, crying, "Paige, Vita's had a relapse. Can you come down?"

Sensing my loss for words, Vita asked: "Did Aunt Nora tell you about Marta?"

"A little," I answered, slipping off my leather jacket and letting it bunch up behind me. "Your aunt told me you've had your hands full. Especially since Richard's death. I'm so sorry, Vita. No one told me he'd died."

Vita's eyes rounded. "You didn't know? God, Paige, I thought you'd abandoned me."

"I sublet my apartment when I started spending more time in Serbia than Toronto. If Nora tried to contact me, I didn't get the message."

Vita slumped back into her pillows. "So how did Aunt Nora find you this time?"

"I was back for a briefing," I answered. "Reuters is sending me to Iraq." An image of me taking Nora's call popped into my head; army boots on my feet, a chador in one hand and a gas mask in the other. I'd been packing my duffle bag with items that might save me should I have to hide amongst the Iraqi women or ward off mustard gas. Because I flew stunt planes in my spare time, I'd been selected to accompany a pilot in an A10 warthog, my assignment, to record a pilot's experience flying the toughest war plane available and to present a bird's eye view of the release and delivery of bombs so high-tech they hone in on the reflected energy of targets. It was pulling me away from my pet project, a book tracing the life of a Serbian woman, Verica Nis, and her family through the barrage of three wars, but my money was running out and this job would hold me for a few more months.

Vita's eyes bored through me for a few seconds. I braced myself, expecting her to go into a tirade on the total uselessness of war the way she'd done in University during the Vietnam War. Back then, I'd believed the United States should send troops in. Now, each time a foreign uprising loomed I had misgivings, but Vita didn't know that. I opened my mouth to tell her, but as quickly as her eyes had penetrated mine, they shifted to the narrow window overlooking the hospital entrance and I realized how far she meant her words, *woes of the world*, to go.

I followed her eyes and looked out at what she couldn't see in that position, a grader removing a new snowfall from the area in front of the hospital entrance. I watched the grader for a few minutes, noting the power the engine needed to push, scoop and lift, and wondered if any engine, other than the fact that I owed her, still powered us.

We'd known each other and kept in touch somewhat for thirty-five years, yet we were totally different. She was a doer; I was a watcher. She was self-reliant and inward; I needed attention and barreled into things. She was gorgeous - tiny, graceful and smiling; I was plain - tall, clumsy and chippy.

Was it perhaps Vita's vulnerable moment on the stairs and my moment of strength that became the catalysts not only for getting us together, but for keeping us together? I wondered if Vita had used her vulnerability as a springboard in her career as a social worker as I so often had used that moment of strength when on assignment in war-torn areas. It's what fired me, made me take risks.

I also wondered what she was expecting when she asked Nora to find me. I certainly couldn't cure the cancer. Did she just want someone who cared near her? Surely she had friends here who were much closer than we were; the bouquets were testimony to that. Perhaps she needed financial assistance. Maybe Richard hadn't purchased adequate insurance coverage, given that they'd only been married a few years. Turning to me for money seemed like a long shot, however, since she had no idea what I earned or if I had any savings.

Vita closed her eyes and looked as if she was trying to fathom a way of asking me for something. This was a familiar look. She'd always had difficulty voicing her needs. She screwed up her lips and remained silent.

Afraid of what she might want, I broke the silence with another apology: "I'm sorry I haven't been available, Vita. I guess I pushed our *keep in touch* promise a little too far this time."

She unhooked her glasses from her ears and let them drop to her chest. They bounced off the stiff surface of her right breast. She trained her eyes on the window again, her brow furrowing into three distinct lines. Two tears slid down her face. She swiped them away. I yanked two tissues out of the Kleenex box on her bedside cabinet and handed them to her. She dabbed at her eyes and blew her nose. "It's just that I've been through so much, Paige."

She picked up her pencil, slipped it into the spiral rings of her notebook and twisted it round and round. Then, she fussed with the white bedding, smoothing everything down. Finally, she swallowed and said, "Can I tell you about Richard?"

I raised my eyebrows and nodded.

She pulled the pencil back out of the spiral binding, drew a circle in the middle of the open page and wrote "Jony" in the centre. She lifted her eyes from the page to mine. They looked bruised. "He was a volunteer for Amnesty International," she began. "When over a hundred Tamil villagers disappeared from the Batticaloa District in Sri Lanka, he became so outraged that he joined an Amnesty contingent to investigate." She tapped the circle. "On the way back to Jaffna, they drove over a Jony mine. If he hadn't been such a bleeding heart, Marta and I would still have him." She turned the page and drew a lopsided heart the entire size of the page. Sighing, she said, "And to think that's what drew me to him in the first place."

This time my eyes rounded. I knew about this. The newspapers had had a heyday with his surname: *Richard Last, Last Seen in Amnesty Convoy; Richard Last in Last Vehicle; Richard Last Performs Last Amnesty Mission.* I hadn't known Richard's full name.

She'd sent a card saying she'd married a man named Richard, the all time best man she'd ever met, who filled all the prerequisites on the list she'd compiled (one that she'd begun in high school after too many disappointing blind dates), but neglected to provide his last name. Her return address showed that she'd kept her maiden name, Alenka. She'd always said she would, to honour her grandmother who'd been her refuge during childhood.

Lost for words again, I got up and arranged the pillows for her. She slid down and pulled the bedding up to her chin. I moved the chair closer to the bed and sat down. She fingered the edge of the sheet with her free hand.

"I really am sorry, Vita," I said, looking down at the scuff marks on the linoleum and checking the black bottoms of my boots to see if they were the culprits.

"You've said you're sorry three times now, Paige. I don't need sorry, I need a friend." She bunched up the sheet in her hand and began kneading it. When she realized what she was doing, she let it go, smoothed it and slid her hand under the blanket. "Can I tell you about Marta now?" she asked.

I nodded and looked up to find her face lighting up. "She's my pride and joy. I adore her. She's dark-skinned and tiny. Her hair curls just like mine and she has adorable dimples in her cheeks." She struggled to sit up and asked me to find an envelope in the drawer of her bed table. She pulled out two photographs. "This is what she looks like now." I looked at a healthy, smiling child, about three years of age, bending to the push of a swing. "She's five," Vita said. She handed me another photo. "This was what she looked like when we got her." I peered at a scrawny child lying in a crib, clad only in a diaper. She looked about a year old. "She was three years old there. She couldn't talk or walk then, and wasn't even potty trained."

"Why?" I asked. "Is she slow?"

A look of incredulity crossed her face. "Oh, Paige, you of all people should know. You've been covering despotic countries, like Romania, for years."

"I'm usually front line, Vita."

"Well, maybe you should branch out. It might take away some of that hard edge of yours." She looked at me straight on this time.

I got up and gazed out the window, wondering why Vita would say that. Hadn't she read anything I'd written over the years? The piece on Tiananmen where I took the student's side, my jubilant reports of the freeing of Russia from Communism and the fall of the wall in East Germany, or my stinging reprisal toward democracies for letting Ethiopia bend to famine? Didn't she see that my hardness was directed at despots and those who allowed - even aided - them to rule? If we were still in school, I'd have called her on it. But we weren't, and now she was too sick to care.

I looked at the pristine picture presented through the hospital window. There, in our dirty world, stood a piece of it looking purer than one might perceive heaven to be: thick white tree limbs bending toward the snow-clad earth; rooftops looking as if someone had stacked cotton batting on them; and clouds of snow edging the parking lot and hospital entrance. Above it all - a sheet of clear blue sky under a sun the colour of buttercups. I thought about the Iraqi skies I'd soon be flying in. Would they be as bright as this? Probably, the desert is rain free most of the time. But then, maybe not, considering the heat waves and sand storms that develop in high temperatures.

Vita's voice cut into my reverie: "You're here, but you're not here, Paige." I swung around to protest, but seeing the lines between her eyebrows deepening, I swallowed the words, sat down on the bed and returned to safe ground. "What about the Romanian orphanages, Vita?"

She gazed at me for a few seconds, I suppose to make sure I'd be listening, and then picked up where she'd left off. "They're hell holes. They're ship-shod structures with meagre budgets. They were set up to house the children Ceausescu ordered people to have in order to increase the working population. When the parents received no subsidies, they abandoned them in hopes that whoever took them in would at least feed them. But the orphanages can't do a proper job, because they're severely understaffed." She held up her index finger. "One caretaker to every thirty children. As a consequence, the kids spend eighteen to twenty hours a day in their cribs. That's why they can't walk. And they aren't talked to or sung to, so they don't learn to mimic words. Besides that, their growth is stunted from malnutrition. Do you know what they're fed?"

I shook my head.

"Water. Bread. And radishes." Her face flushed with indignation. "Even the babies are fed this, mashed up and put into bottles. I had to trick Marta by sneaking fruit and protein between layers of bread, dissolving vitamins in water, and floating radishes in soup. She still can't use a spoon properly. I often have to help her. And, she mustn't eat too much or she'll get sick. Her stomach is smaller than normal because of the tight rations."

I took her hand in mine and asked, "How on earth have you managed?"

"Social Services gave me a leave of absence," she answered. Her fingers tightened around mine for a few seconds then she let go and picked up her pencil. She doodled a sad face in the corner of the "Jony" page. Poor Vita. She had loved her work. She'd specialized in working with single moms and their children, managing at one time to keep more families together than any other case worker in Vernon.

She looked up at the white ceiling and sighed. "And Aunt Nora helps me as much as she can."

"Has it been worth it?" I asked, reaching across her to adjust the pillow that had slipped to her side.

"Every—single—second." Her face lit up again and momentarily erased the worry lines.

A nurse entered just then carrying a tray of paper cups filled with pills. She handed one to Vita. "Well, aren't you looking chipper," she said. "Company must be good for you." She smiled at me as she checked the liquid level in Vita's intravenous bag. "I'll change this next round," she said.

As she left, I turned back to Vita. The ecstatic look on her face had disappeared and she was frantically combing her fingers through her hair in an effort to find the right curl to twist. I remembered her always doing this when distressed. "Paige," she said in a near whisper. "Suppose something happens in my treatment. One of those three women I mentioned, Fiona, she didn't make it. Suppose I don't. Suppose Marta's orphaned again." Her fingers slowed and latched onto a particularly curly lock of hair.

I held my hands out to her. She inched her fingers through her hair, but didn't remove them. I dropped my hands, slid off the bed and began to walk to its foot. As I passed the window, I looked out at the sky again. My pulse quickened and a few butterflies winged around my stomach. To ground myself, I stood at the foot railing and grasped it. Rather than rooting me in the moment, it took me back to the boarding school. "Remember the beds in the dormitory," I said, "white headboards and footboards and white cotton covers like this. Remember how long it took us to line up the two rows of beds the first few times."

"Yes," she said, finally halting her nervous fiddling. "And the missed breakfasts until you admitted having a lazy eye."

I tapped the right hand side of the foot rail. She closed one eye and said, "Two taps on the left, Paige. You do know which one is the left, don't you?" Pleased to have brought back some of her school girl humour, I grinned and gave the two required taps.

"You know, Paige," she said, lying back on her pillows, "I never thought I'd make it in that school. Do you remember the first day?"

"Very well," I said. "We've come a long way."

"Baby," she said in the Virginia Slim context she'd so often mimicked on the rooftop leading out from the shared rooms we'd moved into in the senior grades. She'd rig up *papier mache* cigarette holders in art class when Sister Rosemary was attending to someone else, and later stuff Matinee cigarettes in them and hand them out to anyone who'd brave the roof. Then, she'd don false eyelashes, stilettos and a fringed red shawl and saunter out onto the roof blowing seductive smoke rings. "Baby, baby, baby," she'd say, "y'all have come a long way."

"Do you know how incorrigible you were?" I said, grabbing Vita's toes sticking up from under the blankets. She produced a half grin, the same one she'd given when she nicknamed some of the nuns: The Machine for our overly efficient principal and Buttercup and Bulldog for the personalities and looks of our prefects. I grinned back and gave her toes a shake.

"I wasn't the only one fooling around on the roof," she said. "What about you, opting out of the smoking circle and then jangling a set of rosary beads just outside the door so that we thought Sister Anna Emanuel was about to pounce?"

The mention of the beads brought back a sobering image, The Machine standing beside Vita, fingering the wooden rosary which hung from her waist, while Vita waved goodbye to all the boarders as they piled into various forms of transportation to go home for long weekends and Christmas and Easter holidays.

"You're tough, Vita," I said, spreading my arms and tapping the foot rail on both sides. "You'll come through this with flying colours."

She sighed. "I'm afraid I'm not as tough as you. I've often wished for some of that hard-nosed drive of yours."

I shook the bed slightly. "Hey, a minute ago you wanted me to lose it."

"Oh, you know what I mean. Drive doesn't have to be driven by past wrongs."

Luella and Bridget peeked in just then and asked if Vita could handle more company. Vita motioned them in and patted either side of her bed. I offered my chair so both of them could sit on the same side and slipped into the chair near the door. I studied Luella's curly wig and Bridget's tufts of hair growing back in. These women were obviously veterans of chemotherapy and radiation treatments. I sat back and listened to them speak about ways to alleviate stomach illness and weight loss prior to the treatments. They also spoke of nutrition, advising Vita to drink gallons of orange juice after radiation treatments. As they launched into inviting her to join their support group, the Bosom Buddies, I couldn't help glancing at their chests. Luella had been heavy breasted and would require surgery to build up one side and perhaps reduce the other, and Bridget, who was a small woman, looked as if she'd either had the surgery or found a suitable bra. I had an urge to reach up and cup my healthy breasts in thanksgiving.

I remained still, however, and let myself drift into Vita's observation of my so-called hard-nosed drive and her comment about past wrongs. Was it the latter that motivated me? Was I extending the wrongs of my father, world-wide? And did I seek out violence and fear because that's what I knew? I thought of my stint in the armed forces. I'd easily withstood the humiliating training because it was familiar, the commands replicas of my father's. He had served in Italy in WWII and had returned, I'd been told, a broken man. He took it out on my mother and me, but unlike my mother who bent to his will, I lashed out. Eventually, the same thing happened in the forces. I needed to be a free agent.

But, I also needed the adrenalin rush. I'd been keeping journals while in the army. On re-reading them I found I was fearless in providing detail and had a knack for presenting facts in an interesting manner. Leaving the army and roaming with a pen in place of a gun was a natural progression.

A raucous laugh coming from the two visitors brought me back to the situation at hand. Luella glanced at me and said, "We laugh at ourselves a lot." She turned back to Vita: "And we're active." I realized she was still talking about the Bosom Buddy group.

"Yes," Bridget said. "Right now we're organizing a cancer walk to raise funds for research and up-to-date equipment."

As the women went into detail, I looked down at my size ten feet which had begun a silent tap on the tile. They were itching to get the work done over Iraq and return to Serbia. The last thing they wanted to do was go on a cancer walk. I figured Vita's feet would, though. And, she'd help organize the event despite her current moratorium on the world's woes. Vita was a born organizer. In school, she'd organized a group of girls to lobby for more appetizing meals, glad rags instead of uniforms on weekends and free tennis racquets for those who couldn't afford their own. And she'd gotten them. On the fun side of things in twelfth grade, she negotiated with The Machine to let me out on a week night to attend my boyfriend's graduation dinner. We never told The Machine that my knight in shining tuxedo was protestant.

Since then, I'd heard that she'd lobbied the local government until wheelchair accesses had been installed in all the commercial outlets. She'd rented a wheelchair and wheeled all over town demonstrating the difficulty handicapped people had entering stores and washrooms. It was odd, I thought, how we had to hear about each other from outside sources. We couldn't seem to boast about our accomplishments to each other. Yet, in my case, everything I did was to gain her approval. Was that the case with her too?

When I lifted my eyes from my feet, I saw that Bridget had risen and Luella was stuffing her arms into a down jacket. "Look for us on your doorstep," Bridget said. "We'll be around with broths and nutritional casseroles."

"Yes," Luella said. "Don't even try to cook. It will nauseate you. Just let us look after you for a while."

Vita's eyes brimmed. "What did I do to deserve all this?"

"Not a thing," Bridget said. "Consider it third party payment. People did this for us, and because they aren't sick we can't repay them."

Vita's eyes trailed the swish of the women's skirts out the door. I got up, walked over to her and put my arms around her. She leaned into my shoulder and cried.

I adjusted my face to neutral before moving away from her. This was an automatic response learned long before I took the journalist's road. It went way back to childhood when my father beat the living daylights out of me for having a mind of my own and my mother had stood by, a crushed look on her long face. I'd looked at that face and vowed to keep mine neutral if I wasn't going to do anything about a situation. At the moment, I did it because I hadn't come up with anything concrete to help Vita.

After she'd cried herself out, I moved away from her and patted my blazer pocket to make sure my Marlboro cigarettes were there. I slipped my hand into the pocket and traced the package corner to corner with my index finger.

Vita glanced down at the notepad still perched on her knees. She picked up the pen and slowly drew a series of loops. Then, she scratched them all out. Finally, she said, "There's a tumour in my liver. They found it in the CT scan this morning. That's why I'm so out of sorts."

"What!" I said. I could feel my eyes blinking involuntarily. "How could the cancer have metastasized that quickly?"

"It didn't. I had several lumps in my right breast three years ago. Only the ones that had spread to the fatty issue were removed. The others, I was told, weren't at risk. They should have all been removed."

"Christ!" I said, taking out the cigarette package and turning it over and over.

Vita slumped back onto her pillows. "You'd better not smoke those around Marta," she said. "And for Pete's sake, don't take God's name in vain. Didn't you learn anything when we were kids?"

She closed her eyes and dozed off.

*

In my rented room at the Tiki Village Motel, I tossed my ever-ready suitcase on the stand and sank down onto the bed. I pulled a mickey of Ballantine's out of the case and the cigarettes out of my pocket and stood them side by side on the desk. As I went to the washroom for a glass, Nora's voice resonated: "Paige, you'd better pull on a pair of boots and get up here as fast as you can. Vita's asking for you." I turned to the desk and removed the cellophane from the glass, hearing my own voice, "I can't Nora. I'm on my way to Baghdad." And as I poured the Scotch into the glass and lit a cigarette, Nora's voice re-surfaced: "Well, I can't make you come down, Paige. Before I go, though, do you know anything about a pair of purple sandals? Vita kept mumbling that, along with your name, when she came out of the anesthetic."

I took a gulp of the scotch. Oh yes, I knew. In came the visual, Vita and I huddling together and crossing identical purple sandals over each other. The sound of our resolute voices followed: "We, Paige Colter and Vita Alenka, do solemnly swear to take care of each other until the day we die."

We were eighteen and had just graduated from high school. It was 1968. The oath took place in my father's car. We'd purchased the purple sandals on our way to a beach party at Waskesui Lake in northern Saskatchewan. It was our freedom celebration, not only from school but from the watchful eyes of the nuns. We'd been hyped about going to the resort for months. Many of our school mates spent summers there and talked about it non-stop every September. To get there, I'd somehow caught my father in an expansive mood - likely because I'd landed a summer job at the Saskatoon airport and he no longer had to pay my way – and talked him into lending me his car. At the resort, we checked into a cabin and threw on long flowered skirts and loopy white shawls. We then flip-flopped down to the waterfront in our new sandals. A full moon lit the water and the beach and silhouetted the trees. Fires crackled in fire pits. It felt magical as we joined the partiers around a guitarist and a female singer. Everyone seemed in a festive mood, singing along and swaying to the music. A cigarette was being passed around. Vita and I watched each person take a drag, inhale it deeply, hold it and then slowly release the smoke. Vita poked me in the ribs and whispered, "Are you going to try it?" Ready for anything me grinned and nodded. "You?" I asked. She shrugged.

When it reached us, she took it and immediately passed it on to me. After several cigarettes had been passed, elation washed over me making me feel freer than I'd ever experienced. I began to dance alone to the Beatle's tune, "All You Need Is Love." Everyone moved back and stood in a circle to watch. I crooked my index finger at Vita, but she shook her head and seemed to melt into the crowd. A boy, about my height, 5'11", entered the circle. He was a good dancer and swung me about so deftly I felt like I was one of the dancers in Westside Story. After a few minutes, two other boys, built like boxers, joined us. They danced alone until my partner dropped my hands and motioned to them. They all joined hands and began to circle around me. They moved faster and faster. It made me dizzy. I tried to duck under their arms, but they dipped low barring me from escape.

Suddenly, they stopped circling. One grabbed my wrists and held them while another snatched at my skirt. It had an elastic band and it gave easily. The third boy took my shawl, whooped, swung it around his head and then wound it around me, pinning my arms down.

No one in the circle moved. They were all too stoned to register the danger. Several of them laughed. I felt like the mouse in a game of "Cat and Mouse." Only in this game, there were two circles to escape. I tried to scream but a hand clamped my mouth shut. My dance partner grabbed me and crushed me against his chest. I pushed away but couldn't free myself. The other two boys moved in. All three dragged me toward a thicket of caragana bushes. In the bushes, they threw me down on a pile of branches and ripped off my clothes. The two boxer-types held me down while my dance partner unbuckled his belt.

As I frantically thrashed about trying to free myself, Vita, my scrawny friend, who was six inches shorter than me and thirty pounds lighter, entered the tiny clearing wielding a stick. She yelled "STOP" and hit the boy who was about to violate me across the buttocks. She swung the stick again and hit one of the boys holding me down. "LET HER GO," she yelled. She swung again and hit the third boy on the back.

The boys froze. Seeing a split second chance, Vita grabbed my hand, pulled me up and out of the bushes. We ran like deer across the beachfront and to the car. In the car, she locked the doors, jammed the key into the ignition and spun away, gravel spewing in all directions. When we were far enough away and sure no one was following us, she stopped and pulled out the first aid kit in the glove compartment. As she applied antiseptic ointment on my scratches, I pledged over and over that I'd save her, too, some day.

Now, twenty-three years later, the purple sandal pact had brought me back to save Vita, and I'd stood at the foot of her bed saying nothing helpful and doing even less. I slept very little that night. When I did finally drift off, the telephone rang. It was Nora, panic stricken. "Paige, could you come over and help me out with Marta? She won't move."

I glanced at the clock radio: 5:35 AM.

"All right. Give me an hour."

"Paige, come now. Please."

I tossed my feet over the edge of the bed. "Okay," I said. It wouldn't kill me to go without showering. I'd done it many times in the field, up and out at the crack of dawn to catch jeeps to remote villages and encampments. On those excursions, I'd always been thankful I wasn't a television journalist.

At Nora's, I tried to lift Marta off the bed, but she was dead weight. Nora slumped onto the bed beside her. "She woke up screaming," Nora said. "When I touched her, she went rigid. I couldn't bring her out of it."

"We'll need a doctor, Nora," I said.

She picked up the telephone receiver on the bedside table, but her hand shook so much she couldn't press the over-sized buttons. I sat her down and made the call myself. As I replaced the receiver, I noticed she was trying to tell me something, but couldn't speak. She pointed to a bottle of nitroglycerin beside the telephone and opened her mouth, tongue curled up. I sprayed the medication under her tongue hoping for fast action for both the drug and the ambulance.

In the ambulance, Nora's eyes glazed over. The paramedic, who'd checked her alert bracelet when he arrived, pulled out a lancet and took her blood count. It read 18.6. He looked at me accusingly and filled a hypodermic needle with the insulin he'd picked up from the bedside table. He asked me to bare her midriff for the shot. As I watched the needle sink into her loose flesh and glanced over at Marta in a strait-jacket, because she'd come out of her stupor kicking and threshing, I wondered how many more things could go wrong.

At the hospital, I looked in on Vita while Marta and Nora were being admitted. She was asleep, so I walked down the stairs to the cafeteria. I bought a cup of coffee and selected a boiled egg and toast. The toast was lukewarm and dry but I was so famished I downed it anyway and sat there clutching my coffee with both hands to warm them. I closed my eyes and thought about my dilemma; here I was in this sleepy town attempting to tend to an old friend and her family, while I was itching to board a plane. What value could I be in such a mind-set?

What about this friendship? Did it all boil down to that promise made years ago? We had so little in common anymore.

Vita, the all-caring one, seemed to find fulfillment in belonging to one community where she could become familiar with local issues and do something concrete about them. I, the selfish, unsettled one needed to take on the world. She wanted stability and family and a house with a garden. I'd forfeited all semblance of normality. I'd had two husbands and a string of lovers, but couldn't stay in one place long enough to please any of them. I had no children. I didn't even have a fixed address. If I needed a place for a while, I borrowed or sublet from other journalists also on the prowl.

The word *prowl* settled on me. Yes, I was like a lioness or tigress always moving, always looking for my next meal.

I picked up my cup, refilled it and took it outside. I brushed the snow off a corner of the table, set the coffee down and pulled out my cigarettes. As I tapped one out, I heard the sound of a jet and tried to locate its stream in the murky sky. The impulse to leave shot through my body and settled in my gut. I lit my cigarette eyeing a waiting taxi at the hospital entrance. I smoked the cigarette down to the filter battling the question: What if Vita, slight as she was, had only been concerned with her own safety when no one moved out of that circle to help me? I ground the cigarette out with the toe of my boot and met the anticipatory eyes of the taxi driver. I shuffled my feet in the snow. A breeze came up just then and knocked snow off a tree and into my hair. It gave me a chill. I shivered and looked at the driver again. I took several steps toward him then stopped, bit my bottom lip and held it. "Not yet," I said. I returned to the hospital entrance to begin calling all the care facilities I could find in the telephone book.

After coming up with nothing but answering machines, I slipped into the children's ward to look in on Marta. She was lying perfectly still in a crib. "Why is this child in a crib?" I asked. "She's five years old."

"Safety reasons," the nurse answered. A puzzled look crossed her face. "Funny, she settled right down when we put her in it."

Later, when I wheeled Vita down to the children's ward, I asked her if Marta still slept in a crib." Instead of answering me, she twisted back and looked up at me, her nose crinkling. "Paige, those cigarettes you smoke smell like cigars. Could you at least wash your hands afterward?" I lifted my left hand off the wheel chair handle and smelled it. It was rank. No doubt my clothes were, too. When I flew through New York to Toronto, I'd picked up a carton of Marlboro cigarettes, my favourite while I lived in the States.

I parked the chair by the washroom and went in to wash my hands. When I came out, I asked about the crib again.

"Yes, when Marta feels threatened," she said. "The bars on the crib make her feel safe." She turned forward and looked straight ahead until we reached Marta's bedside. She took one look at Marta's listless body and cried, "She's drugged, Paige. I can't believe it. I've managed her all this time without drugs." She stroked the child's face over and over in an attempt to bring her around.

I'd been all for the drugs, anything to quiet the kid. "So, what do you do to subdue her?"

"I don't let her get this far. I watch for signs of agitation. Sometimes I hold her for hours. All her reactions are caused by fear. You can smell it on her. It's best to make her feel safe. Anything can set her off, even something as subtle as smell, sound, taste, or change of body temperature. Aunt Nora knows this, but her health is too poor right now to pay such close attention."

I didn't know it at the time, but those few sentences were to become the most important ones I'd ever listened to.

Marta and I have had a rough time. Vita's death negated what had been done to pull Marta out of her half-monkey state to walking and talking. Although she was five years old, she moved about by rolling or sliding on her bottom, and she crouched behind furniture, sucking her thumb voraciously whenever I tried to touch her or get her to co-operate. She still has a big callus on the crook of her thumb. In addition, she constantly wet herself and insisted on changing her own Pamper panties. Cleanliness became an issue. I was beside myself until one day Marta picked up a feather duster I'd left on the floor with the dustpan and caressed her face with it. Vita's words then surfaced: "She was never touched gently, Paige. At first, she'd only let me touch her face with something soft." I washed the duster that night and kept it handy. After a few days of playing with it herself, she began removing it from its hook and handing it to me. Eventually, she allowed me to stroke her cheeks with my fingertips the way Vita used to do. And, after six months of hit and miss bathing, she finally let me give her a good scrub.

Vita had stressed the importance of stability for Marta, so I vowed to move only once. Vita's insurance policy covered Marta's expenses, but I had to find work to keep myself going. The Calgary Herald hired me to cover local affairs and human interest stories. It's rather lame in comparison to international assignments. Sometimes I want a different life, but this pays the bills and the occasional scandal or sting operation keeps me somewhat interested.

Moving to Calgary was an ordeal. I tried using her wheelchair to board the plane, but Marta locked the wheels and I couldn't pry her hands off the brakes. I had to summon a doctor to give her a tranquilizer. To make matters worse, the plane had engine trouble and had to land in a field near Banff. By the time it was repaired, Marta had wakened and refused to re-board. I ended up having to arrange a ride to Banff where I rented a car to complete the trip. She didn't buck over riding in cars, so I realized that young as she was when she flew to Canada the residual memory must not have been a good one.

In our Calgary apartment, Marta slid around the rooms on her bottom, whimpering. I left the door open to bring in our things and she slipped out into the hallway. She shrieked when she found it led nowhere. Later, when she spoke again, she said, "I just wanted to find Mommy's flower garden." She was referring to Vita's room which was decorated with floral wallpaper. She told me that she and Nora had helped Vita plant the garden on the walls.

When Vita couldn't waken Marta, she agreed to look in on Nora in the outpatient ward. We found her calm enough to leave. "She must not have any more upsets, though," the doctor said. He looked at me, not Vita. "You'll need to arrange care for the child."

Back in Vita's room, I asked, "Do you think Bridget or Luella could help with Marta?"

She shook her head.

"Anyone else, Vita? Perhaps one of those people who sent flowers?"

"Those are from my co-workers and clients." She pursed her lips and thought a moment: "Maybe Liza, my neigbhour, at night and on the weekends. She's a little familiar with Marta's problems." She pulled her list out from under her pillow and added "Call lawyer" to it. "You'd better go get Nora," she said, sinking into her pillows. Her face was so flushed that I reached out and touched her forehead. It was burning hot. "It's these awful headaches," she said.

I rushed out to the Nurse's Station to get attention for Vita and then downstairs to the Outpatient ward to fetch Nora.

At Nora's, I prepared a can of beef and barley soup and a toasted cheese sandwich. Nora picked out the solid bits and put them on the plate. She then asked me to pour the broth into a cup. She drank that, but left the sandwich. I wrapped it in Saran Wrap and set it beside her teapot for later. She tried to smile, but began to cry instead. "What will happen to that child?" she questioned.

After several minutes of sobbing, I relented: "I'll take her to Vita's and stay with her for a while," I said. My voice sounded as if it belonged to someone else. I remained with her until she pulled herself together. Before leaving, I entered my page number onto her telephone call list and the number for the hospital and Home Care.

Marta was dressed and sitting in a wheel chair when I returned to the hospital. "Hello, Marta," I said. "Would you like to visit your mother?" Her eyes leapt and her head nodded. As yet, I hadn't heard her speak. I reached out to pat her shoulder, but she shrank away from my hand and attempted to turn the wheels on the chair. I scooted around the chair and released the brake. She put both hands on the wheels and propelled it forward. She'd obviously been in one before. "You need one with a motor on it," I said, guiding the chair toward the hallway and into the elevator.

"I rode one once," she said.

Whoa! I thought. The kid can talk. Maybe it won't be so bad after all. I asked her where she'd ridden one, but the door opening on the opposite end of the elevator captured her attention.

In Vita's room, Marta scrambled out of the chair and tried to climb up on the bed. It was too high. I came up behind her and said, "I'll give you a lift." She hesitated, but gave in, the desire being stronger than the method this time.

Vita opened her arms and the child fell into them. She dug her fingers into Vita's arms jarring the IV needle. Vita winced. I moved forward to pull her off, but Vita said, "She'll slacken in a few seconds." She did.

When Marta settled into Vita, back against her torso, I touched Vita's forehead. "I see your fever's down."

She nodded and pointed to the IV. "Miracle drugs." She stroked Marta's face and kissed her on the top of her head.

I busied myself with straightening the bed linen over the two of them. Then, I poured a glass of water from the thermos and placed it on the stand on Vita's left. Finally, I said, "If you give me your keys, I'll take Marta home for a few days."

"Oh, would you?" she said, a huge smile springing up and melting her reserve. "She'd be so pleased to be with her own things." She buried her face in Marta's thick curls.

Marta squirmed and said, "I stay here, Mommy."

As I left the room to retrieve Vita's keys at the Nurse's station, I heard Vita making a pitch to convince Marta to go with me: "You can go home and see your teddy bears and dollies. I'll bet your favourite bear, Moses, is very lonely, and I can hear your Wet-um doll, Mary, crying for you to come and change her."

While I waited for the keys, a stroke of genius hit me - I would rent a motorized wheel chair. The desk attendant called a Medic Supply store and was promised a delivery in ten minutes. "You'll need transportation," she said, and arranged for Handy Dart to pick us up in forty-five minutes.

To kill time, I wandered into the lounge at the end of the hall. A patient and his wife were sitting there watching television. I sat down near the door and looked the man over. His legs were in casts and his head was wrapped in a mummy-like bandage. Purple blotches were forming beneath his eyes. I imagined him in a street or barroom brawl. I glanced at the woman and noticed a look that said *I don't need this*. I wondered if my face was reflecting the same message to her.

The wheelchair arrived early. I tramped out to pay the attendant and ask him to teach me the intricacies of the thing. Then, I sat in it and rode down the hall. When I entered the room, Vita laughed and clapped her hands. Marta stared at me as I whipped around in circles several times. I got out, set the brake and spoke to Vita, hoping Marta would sidle over to the chair. She didn't.

"You can give me a ride," Vita said. She disentangled herself from Marta and asked me to swing the IV pole around to the chair so that she could get out of bed. When she sat in the chair, Marta scrambled off the bed, too, and hopped onto Vita's knees. I watched this maneuver wondering if I could think of something as simple and as effective as that.

At the elevator, Marta surprised both of us by switching to the seat by herself. The button pressing was such a novelty she wanted to keep going. Vita grabbed the IV pole for support and waved us off. I stopped on every floor and let Marta ride in the halls. Outside, she wheeled up and down the sidewalk until Handy Dart arrived. The van's ramp intrigued her. "I do it myself," she said and rode on without a struggle. Point one for me, I thought, and gave the driver a thumbs up signal.

When we arrived home, she ran to her room and sat on the floor amongst her toys. She didn't play with them, just sat there. I found a package of Lipton's Chicken Noodle Soup and prepared it. Comfort food from my childhood. I ladled a bowl for each of us and put two ice cubes in hers. That, too, I remembered from childhood. It occurred to me that my mother and perhaps most mothers had to trust their instincts with children. I put the soup on the table, and called Marta to come and eat. She remained in her room. I tried to cajole her by promising ice cream for dessert. Not a flicker of movement. I gave in and telephoned Nora.

"Take the soup to her room and feed her," she said.

"On the floor?"

"Yes. She doesn't eat normally, Paige. Didn't Vita tell you that?"

"Come to think of it, she did."

"Also, don't give her too much. She'll overeat and become sick."

"She told me that, too," I said, admonishing myself for not paying closer attention. I took the soup into Marta's room and sat down on the floor. She slurped it out of the spoon as if she hadn't eaten for a long while. When finished, she got up, ran to the refrigerator and tried to open it. "Radish," she screamed. "Radish. Radish." I opened the door. She grabbed at a plastic container, pulled it forward, and toppled it to the floor. The second I opened it, she dipped her hand in, grabbed a handful of radishes and ran back to her room.

At bedtime, I was clearly no substitute for Vita. Marta swung from bed to crib a dozen times during the night in spite of her assertion, "I big girl," when being tucked into the single bed. Vita had told me she slept with Marta when she was too restless, but Marta would have nothing to do with me. I spent the night listening to the rattle of crib rails and her night fright screams. I was ragged by morning and ready to spank her little bottom. Isn't that what my mother did? I reflected on this for a moment and soon sobered to the fact that my mother's instincts hadn't been great. She'd spanked me for hiding from my father when he was in a rage. I always ended up getting two whippings and sent to my room. When I came out, I was more belligerent than when I went in.

I called Vita's neighbour, Liza, for help. "I'm not equipped for this," I said.

"I'm so sorry," she said, "but we're leaving for Mexico today. We're just packing up the car now."

I hung up, dropped my elbows on the counter and leaned so far forward my forehead touched the cold, green Arborite on the counter top. The coolness calmed me enough to respond to the shrill ring of the telephone. It was Nora.

"Paige, the hospital called." Her voice quivered. "Vita's in trouble. She can't speak. They're taking her down for a brain scan."

I took a deep breath. "Just…where…are…we…headed?" I said. There was silence on the other end. I stood there for a minute with the receiver in my hand, then hung up and shifted into the only mode I felt comfortable with, action.

"Marta, time to get up," I yelled as I pulled breakfast items out of the refrigerator. There was no response, so I went into her room. "You need to get dressed," I said. "We're going to see Mommy." I took a set of purple slacks, a white shirt and a pair of matching socks out of the bureau and reached over the crib rails to pull her pajama top off. She screamed. I backed away, leaving the clothes in the crib. A few minutes later, she came out dressed in green overalls and a yellow shirt. Her socks were red and mismatched in design. Oh, well, I thought, and popped two pieces of bread into the toaster.

Marta grabbed the loaf of bread off the cupboard, pulled out two more pieces, and pointed to an apple in the fruit bowl. "Slice," she said.

I sliced the apple on the rounded side and handed a piece to her. She stamped her feet. "No. Wrong way."

As I grabbed another apple out of the fruit bowl, I thought, Christ, am I going to do anything right? Voice harsh, I asked, "Which way?" She backed away a little, but pointed to the stem. Not wanting a repeat of the previous day, I refrained from slashing through the apple and ever so controlled cut a thin slice off and removed the seeds from the middle. Marta reached up to the cutting board for it, placed it on one piece of the bread and covered it with the other.

"Samich," she said, looking victorious.

I toasted the two slices of bread sitting in the toaster and made myself a sandwich with the "wrong way" apple slices. I poured milk for both of us. She promptly spilled hers. Agitated, I wiped it up thinking it's a damn good thing you didn't have kids of your own.

When finished, I said, "Now, let's brush our teeth." That, too, was an ordeal. I used Total instead of the children's toothpaste. I turned the tap on instead of putting water in a glass. And I used the wrong toothbrush. There was a Barney one I hadn't noticed.

By the time we caught the Handy Dart and drove the wheelchair up to Vita's room in the hospital, Vita was back from the testing. She looked awful, hair brushed up in several spots, skin taut around her eyes. And she still couldn't speak. Her eyes were wild with fear. I located her notepad and pencil and gave it to her.

"I have a brain tumour, as well," she wrote.

"How big?" I asked.

"Big," she wrote. "They can't operate."

Marta wiggled out of the chair. Vita motioned to help the child up on the bed. Marta curled up against Vita the same way she had the day before. When she relaxed, so did Vita. I watched this settling in as if nothing could be more natural, and felt very much like an extra player who hadn't memorized the moves or the lines. I turned away and looked out the window. An erratic breeze caught some loose snow and swirled it in the air, then fizzled out letting the snow sift to the ground. In the sky, the sun and clouds seemed at odds over which one would have jurisdiction – light spotting an apartment window here and there, clouds casting a dull hue on the snow laden branches of the poplar trees.

I shifted my gaze back to Marta and Vita. Vita was drawing pictures of animals on her notepad. Marta named them and Vita wrote the names under the pictures. She tore the pages off, clumsily assembled the pictures into a booklet and pulled out a stapler from the drawer in the swing table. She fumbled with the stapler. Frustrated, she looked to me for help. I stapled the pages together and handed Marta a box of crayons.

While Marta coloured, Vita picked up her pencil and wrote, "I'm not going to make it, Paige. They've cancelled the chemotherapy treatments." Tears spilled onto her cheeks. Her eyes darted to Marta. She wiped away the tears and took big gulps of air in an effort to gain control. When she calmed down, she wrote, "When do you have to go to Iraq?" I looked out the window at the clouds, now dark enough and plump enough to give birth to more snow, and then back at Vita. Her face reflected the darkness outside. I crossed my arms behind my back and walked the length of the room several times. Finally, I stopped at Vita's bedside, took the pen and pad from her and wrote, "I think I'll skip this assignment."

I looked out the window again and saw that the snow had begun to fall. It came down in huge white flakes. Vita's eyes followed mine. She took the pad from me and wrote, "Angel wings." The smile she gave me was beatific.

Marta, fourteen years old now, looks well fed, but small for her age. At the moment, she's looking at a three-fold picture frame containing a photo of herself on the left, she and Vita in the middle, and she and I on the right.

The solo picture depicts her at four years old wearing red Osh Kosh overalls and yellow boots. The boots are unlaced as if she'd been trying to take them off, but didn't quite make it before someone said, "Stand straight and smile."

In the middle photograph, Marta sits on Vita's knees in a denim dress and pink sandals. Marta's hand lies on Vita's wrist. Both wrists are fine-boned. Their splayed fingers are slender and long. Vita's skin has a pink tone, while Marta's is olive coloured, but they both possess heads of dark, curly hair and large chocolate brown eyes. At first glance, you'd swear they were mother and daughter.

The third picture looks awkward. I, tall, red-headed and big-boned dwarf Marta at 4'10"and very slender. My face, square and framed by a blunt haircut contrasts with her pixie-like face surrounded by a shock of long black hair which is almost straight. Her hair is curly, but she doesn't like it, so I've taught her Vita's trick of spreading her hair out on an ironing board and recruiting someone to iron out the waves for her.

Marta's room is large and bright. French doors lead out to a balcony overlooking the Bow River. A skylight allows the sunshine in above a tiny loft. A yellow canopy hangs over white turned posts on the bed frame. An antique dresser we found at an auction and painted white stands against the opposite wall. Marta haunts pawn shops and collectable shops for ethnic things. A Turkish rug lies in front of the bed and her dresser sports knobs she ordered from a Romanian ceramic dealer. The books on her shelf all have the word Romania in them. It's as if she can only accept the present if she can somehow touch her past.

As I've mentioned, Marta is a tiny girl. Her arms are long, however, almost reaching her knees. And her fingers are like delicate china hanging below them. She opens and shuts them a lot. The psychologist says it's a subconscious movement which seems to ground her. He wonders if she'd slept in a hammock and used her arms to stabilize herself. I don't know. I do know she liked being in a crib. She was seven years old by the time she gave it up.

One thing she's never given up is her stubbornness. She rails against anything she feels is unjust. At home, she rages whenever she feels I'm dictating rather than reasoning. And in school, she walks out of class when, in her opinion, unfair rules or comments arise. She did it just last week, after being chastised for inattention. When I chased her down, she said, "I couldn't answer his questions because I didn't understand them, not because I wasn't listening. He wasn't listening when I tried to explain."

Marta's behind children her own age. She's only in grade 7. I've hired numerous tutors and counselors to get her to this point. It took a year for her to begin speaking again and she transported herself on her behind even longer. She was eight years old before she could handle a fork and she constantly injured herself by falling down. If asked her age, she always says, "I'm twelve." It prevents teasing and because she's so small she gets away with it. She seldom invites anyone over, preferring to sit in the rocker in her room reading. She now has more statistics about Romania jammed into her head than a state diplomat.

This fixation makes me think Marta's almost ready to learn the details of her adoption. Amongst Vita's belongings, there is a journal describing it.

I brought Vita home on Jan. 15th. The operation on her lymph nodes had healed and she'd been stabilized with heavy doses of Prednisone. Her speech returned, but it was often garbled. The medication caused her head to swell to twice its size and to give her false energy. She'd jump out of bed and clean like a woman possessed then fall back into bed, exhausted.

She refused to see anyone, preferring to devote her time to Marta. When she could speak clearly enough, she repeatedly told me she wouldn't wish her affliction on anyone. She thanked me dozens of times for staying.

January gave in to February. The war in Iraq, which came into fruition just after I'd promised to stay, continued. Thousands of bombs were being dropped on weapon's arsenals and communication centres. I kept track of the A10 warthogs being flown three times a day and their dead-on hits. Newscasters reported how difficult these planes were to fly and how pilots dreaded them at first. No one was assigned to replace me in the cock-pit of one, my one consolation.

I kept media notes and stayed in touch with Reuters and a few government sources. I also free-lanced for *The Kelowna Courier*, writing feature stories on whatever struck me. I wrote one on the callous way cancer patients were informed of their eventual demise, charging that doctors handled the situations this way to avoid being sued later by family members. It was syndicated and circulated Canada-wide. I received a lot of affirmative feedback from families of cancer victims, and flack from the medical profession. This made me realize that even local stories were of value.

All the while, Vita obsessed over cleaning. It was as if having a clean home would give her a clean bill of health. In addition, she began a new ritual, letter writing. I noticed, as I posted them, that they were all addressed to a lawyer named Edward Chu. After numerous postings, I asked her about them. She was in the living room wielding a dust rag on the oak furniture. "I'm trying to look after my affairs like the doctor suggested," she said. I pushed further asking who she'd named to care for Marta. She shook her head, crouched down in front of the coffee table and vigorously dusted the oak wood, concentrating on a bleached spot in the middle. She poured Lemon Pledge on her rag and rubbed the spot over and over. "We can't find any family," she said, finally. There was a long pause before she stopped rubbing, looked up at me and tentatively added, "I've been kind of hoping you'd take her."

I was so taken aback that I retorted, "I can't, Vita."

Her eyes bore through me. I raised my eyes to hers and found in them a look that said *I'll fall on my knees if I have to.*

I looked away. How could she ask me to do this? This was far beyond our pact.

Sinking down on the sofa facing the table, I folded my hands on my lap and trained my eyes on them. I couldn't look at Vita. The hope I'd seen in her eyes and on her anguished face made me squirm. "Vita, you know that my job takes me all over the world," I reasoned. "And that I don't even have a home to take her to. You also know how ill-suited I am to parent. What if I bash her around like my father bashed me?"

I could feel Vita's unwavering eyes still on me. In a low, almost inaudible tone, she said, "You wouldn't do that. Because you're aware of the possibility."

I jumped up, nearly knocking the bottle of furniture polish over. "It's out of the question, Vita," I said.

Vita's breath caught. She picked up the polish and capped it tight, almost breaking the top. "I wouldn't ask you if I had an alternative," she said. "If Marta goes to the state, she'll get lost in the system; I've seen it happen dozens of times. No one will adopt her. She'll get shifted from foster home to foster home. Problem children always do."

She stood up, went to the kitchen and put the polish away. I slumped onto the sofa and stared at the white spot on the table. I'll put a bowl on it, I thought. I searched my mind wondering if I'd seen a suitable one in Vita's cupboards. Maybe the crimson one in the china cabinet. Yes, I thought, that one, but I couldn't make myself stand up to go get it.

Vita stopped cleaning that day. She took to her bed and began sleeping most of the time. The sleep, it turned out, was a coma which she dipped in and out of. I realized, then, that her cleaning frenzy was not only drug-induced but driven by need.

She had very few lucid moments after that. In addition, the pain became unbearable. She winced and cried out, even in her sleep. Her doctor ordered the administration of morphine through an IV. A home care nurse, named Andrea, set it up and monitored it twice a day. Within a few weeks, her liver stopped functioning causing fluids to accumulate. Her abdomen swelled so much she appeared pregnant under the blankets. To relieve it, Andrea drained the bile with a siphon-like apparatus.

During Marta's naps, which took place on Vita's bed when total exhaustion took over, I sat beside Vita longing for the days when all we had to speculate about was John Lennon and Paul McCartney coming to pluck us out of that religion-sopped convent and transport us to locales like Penny Lane or Abbey Road. I longed for the arguments because they always taught us something new about the world or about us. And I longed for those arm-hooking times when we walked over Saskatoon's 25th Street bridge to the

University campus where we'd stare at the stone buildings and question what wonders awaited us. All that, yet we'd let time tear us apart. And now this time together, but only in spirit. And was it in spirit? Vita wasn't conscious most of the time. And did I not still long to be back in Kosovo writing my book?

I thought of Andrea, the home care nurse telling me, "Dying is beautiful. It's a time of coming full circle and of drawing in, determining what's important. And it's a time to make peace with your maker so you can pass joyfully into the next realm." I wondered if Vita, in the condition she was in, was actually doing this. I also wondered why we'd been chosen to get a spiritual nurse. Then I remembered Vita's naming of Marta's toys, Moses for the teddy bear and Mary, the doll, and realized that while my experience covering godforsaken political disputes had induced me to repudiate Christian doctrine, Vita had remained a solid devotee. Whether or not she made peace with the maker she believed in didn't matter at this point.

Nora, too, spoke like the nurse and seemed able to soothe Vita. Because of this and because Nora's health had eroded so much that I was shifting from house to house, I moved her in with us. Marta was delighted. So was I as she kept the child company. Marta hadn't taken to me at all and found ways to let me know: stamping her feet when I didn't do things exactly as Vita had, giving me an evil eye when I asked her to put her toys away, and constantly whining and climbing all over Vita, leaving her wincing with pain. I'd had to bar her from going into Vita's room a good deal of the time and was rewarded with severe temper tantrums. I had no idea how to handle a child lying prostrate on the floor, kicking and screaming. Nora didn't either, but the familiarity of her and her lavish love and attention settled Marta down somewhat.

Unfortunately, Nora suffered a stroke within a month of arriving and was once again hospitalized. It was a big blow for Marta. She wondered around the house like a tiny lost animal whimpering and calling Nora's name, and hauling out toys for her to play with. I was at a loss.

When Nora returned home, I found myself running instead of walking. It was so harrowing that I began to spin the days out in a haze. I got up and dressed in the clothes I'd brought not noticing that they were beginning to wear. I served the food Luella and Bridget continued to leave on the doorstep, but couldn't remember what we'd had five minutes after leaving the table. I smoked pack after pack of cigarettes often leaving them lit in ashtrays, my kind of ash trays, empty tuna fish cans. Luckily, I had to keep them outside as Vita could smell smoke even in the drugged state she was in.

I became so edgy that I decided it best to put Marta into a child care facility part-time. She howled when I left her, but the care worker said she could handle it. Each day, when I returned for Marta, she was always in a crib curled up and sucking her thumb. Her face and body looked spent. I suspected she'd been having tantrums, but didn't dare ask the care-giver for fear of having to withdraw her. Often, I was too spent myself and would just sit beside her and watch her suck her thumb. At these times, I questioned Vita's wisdom in wanting to die at home.

On Vita's final morning, Andrea drew me aside shortly after coming in. "She's hanging on by a thread, Paige," she said. "Perhaps you should ask the doctor to increase the morphine." I checked the monitor to see how long it would be until more was needed. Her only lucid moments occurred when it had run low.

"I'll ask her," I said. She looked skeptical.

Marta trundled in carrying the quilt Vita had made for her before her arrival. I lifted her onto the bed and tucked her beside Vita. Then, I took my usual place at the foot of the bed and pulled the bedding back to massage Vita's feet. Andrea had advised this. "Sometimes a cancer patient can tolerate her feet being touched when she can't stand it anywhere else," she'd said. She'd also shown me how to perform Reiki, healing touch without touching. Its purpose was to massage the energy field around Vita. These rituals were the only things I could do and I'd been doing them faithfully. Now, as I touched the bottom of her feet, Vita's eyes opened slightly then clamped shut again. I worked gently, trying to warm her feet with my hands. They were colder than usual, like stones just thrown on shore by the sea.

Cold! Stones! I stopped short. "Cold feet," Andrea had said, "are a sign of near death."

I reached for Vita's wrist. There was a beat, albeit rather slow. I resumed the massage checking Vita's breathing every few seconds. As I gazed into her weary face, I wished I could do more for her. Then I looked at Marta tucked in beside her and realized I was watching a scene as poignant as the Pieta in the Basilica. In all of my travels, that was the one image which stayed with me - the love between mother and child, something I'd craved and never received. Overcome with something I couldn't name, I tried to will Vita's eyes open. I succeeded, not just the usual slit of white, but open wide, the gold in them shining like polished topaz. And although she hadn't been able to speak for weeks, she said my name and Marta's in a clear voice.

I grasped her ankles and closed my eyes. My mouth opened and the words, "I'll look after her for you," slipped out.

When I opened my eyes, Vita's still face was bathed in a shaft of light from a burst of late afternoon sun. Another shaft of light struck Marta's sleeping face.

It's a lovely thing, this journal, hand-embossed on natural paper with pressed purple violets winking out from under a plastic covering. I take off the plastic and finger the rough paper, the delicate flowers. I leave it like this. It feels closer to Vita somehow, raw like she was, yet always blossoming, even to the end.

When I give it to Marta, she holds it delicately, then gives me a withering look as if to say how could you have kept this from me? I return the look, having received it once too often. As I watch her turn and stalk out of the room stepping hard like Vita used to do when determined, I finally admit to myself that the roots I'd tried so hard to establish for Marta are as tangled as the ones she arrived in Canada with.

Marta bumps into the rocking chair in her room. She's always clumsy when upset. I hear her fall into the chair. The floor squeaks as she rocks. I go to my study to finish an article on teenage suicide in the remote communities of northern Alberta. As I research the material I've gathered, I glance at Marta's door hoping I haven't triggered yet another problem. Is she too withdrawn? I ask myself. Is she strong enough to handle the truth about her adoption? Spurred by the subject matter I'm writing about, I begin an inventory of what I store in my medicine cabinet and the kitchen drawers. I try to remember if there's any rope in the storage cupboard, knowing that wouldn't matter because kids have been known to pull cords from parkas in public places until enough could be strung together.

The paper's deadline looming, however, I force myself to let go of all that and let my professional training take over. Concentration on the subject to the exclusion of all else. Speed. Accuracy. I bury myself so deep in it that I don't hear Marta enter the room. She touches my shoulder and says, "Mom".

Startled, I swing my chair around. "You always call me Paige."

"Well, I guess you're the mother I know best." She hands me the journal.

"You don't remember your mother as she is in this journal?"

She shakes her head. "I'm a gypsy," she says. Her voice sounds bewildered. "It was the gypsies who left children in the street."

"You can't be sure of that, Marta. There were a lot of poor families who couldn't look after their children."

She leaves the room. I hear her dragging a chair to her bookshelves and pulling down a book. She brings it in to me and flips the pages to a section about the numerous children left on streets by gypsies. She then flips open the journal to a page she'd put a book mark in. The passage reads: "Richard returned from Romania today. He brought a picture of a little girl, named Marta, who was found in the streets of Bucharest. She has large brown eyes with thick black lashes and curly black hair. She's thin beyond thin and her eyes are forlorn. They're like the eyes we've seen in starving African children. Her skin looks quite dark or olive coloured. I'd almost swear she has some African or Indian blood in her."

I look into Marta's tiny triangular face and reach for her hand. She pulls back, but changes her mind and lets me envelop it. It's clammy and cold. I take both her hands to warm them. "Do you want to try to find out?" I ask.

She nods. "I called you Mom because my adoptive mother didn't even want me."

"What makes you say that?" I ask. She picks up the journal and points to the next section: "Richard wants to adopt her. He says she's the only one who grabs the bars of her crib, raises herself and bangs on the bars. He figures she's a survivor. I'm not so sure I want to do this. Perhaps we should wait for a Canadian baby."

"*Have you read further?*" *I ask.*

She shakes her head. "*I can't read anymore of it right now.*"

"*If that's the case, then I'm going to tell you about your mother.*" *I tell her about her condition when Vita and Richard adopted her and how Vita dropped everything, including her career, to focus on her recovery and development. I tell her about how Vita hung onto life until sure her little girl was looked after. And I mention how difficult it must have been for her after Richard was killed and she had to do everything alone.*

"*I wish Dad hadn't died. He's the one who rescued me, really.*"

"*Yes, he did, but it was your mother who got you to walk and talk and eat nutritious food. And she's the one who lavished enough love on you to rescue ten children.*"

"*I feel like everyone leaves me. I think you even want to leave me.*"

I think of the look we'd exchanged earlier and of all the times she'd lurked at my office doorway, saying, "*You miss doing stories in other countries, don't you?*" *Then, I think of Vita telling me that stability is the one thing Marta must have. The word turns over and over in my mind:* "*Stability. Stability. Stability.*" *Finally, I shut away Vita's voice, thinking, you're not here Vita, and you don't know if that's still applicable, and I drop Marta's hands to hold my arms out to her.* "*If you're a gypsy,*" *I say,* "*perhaps you should be moving about from place to place. And perhaps I, too, am a kind of gypsy. Suppose you and I wrap scarves around our heads, buy long cotton skirts and go a-wandering. We could start with British Columbia and wend our way to Romania to see what we can find out about you.*"

Marta enters my arms, throws her arms around me and giggles into my shoulder. As I bask in my first real connection with this child, I visualize the purple sandals Vita and I crossed over each other, and hear our earnest voices promising to look after each other for the rest of our lives. A tingling sensation courses through my body. I snuggle Marta closer to me and whisper, "*Maybe, just maybe, you and I now have a story to tell.*"

THE CHAIR

His nephews, Theo and Frank, pull his Lazy-boy chair apart. It is too large to get through any of the doors, so they pound and rip and pile up the pieces at the back door. No one has consulted him on this.

They open the back door and haul the chair pieces out, through the garden and into the back alley. He traces their steps down the plank walk and tries to hold the gate closed with his mind. He realizes it is futile. They probably couldn't put the chair back together, anyway. He has felt every rip of the chair in his own frame. Wishes it was over. Wishes they would pull him apart and be done with it.

He has lung cancer and the doctors have told him to go home and live each day one at a time. His wife, Arlene, and daughter, Karla, refuse to accept this. They are sure his life can be prolonged if they administer oxygen at the moment of need, cook him chicken and dumplings and rhubarb pie, and give him a new smooth chair to sit in. "That old thing wasn't comfortable enough, George," Arlene says. "Not to sit in for so many hours. It was terribly lumpy." When she sees him staring at the empty space, she says, "We wanted to surprise you, but Karla and I couldn't move the old chair ourselves. We're lucky Theo and Frank came by today. Your new chair will come tomorrow. It's a navy blue Lazy-boy with a massager. You're going to love it."

He wants to inquire why she didn't ask him first, but when he looks into her eyes and sees the caring in them, he realizes she is just trying her best. All the same, he wishes she and everyone piled into this house right now would have left his chair alone. It had been with him for years. Had the curve of his buttocks in it. Rocked to his body rhythm. Reacted smoothly to his hand on its handle. He will not have time to break in a new chair.

He hears the bump of the last piece of wood against the door and remembers the bump the delivery men from Simpson Sears gave the chair when they entered that door some twenty years ago. He recalls cutting away the plastic, slowly and methodically, as he was prone to do when savouring something, and running his hands across the back and down the arms. It reminded him, then, of examining a horse prior to buying it. And when the foot rest yawned upward, he had smiled, thinking of the horse's jaws he so frequently opened to check gums and teeth.

As he had sat down in the chair, it felt unwieldy, like the flanks of an unbroken horse. It made him think of Tom, a horse he had purchased in his youth. The previous owner claimed Tom had been broken, but anyone looking into those huge wild eyes knew Tom would never completely submit to anyone. That was why he bought him. And that was why this chair appealed to him; it was something new and frisky, like Tom. He thought it would never yield to his commands. But, as the years went by, it swayed to his shape and its foot rest lever readily accepted his hand. He almost wished it would balk a little, arch its back and try to throw him. After a while, he believed it had yielded to him because its freedom was in the ride.

He cannot imagine owning a new chair at this stage of his life, when only the worn and familiar mean anything to him. Lumpy indeed! He had already spent a good deal of time in that old chair. Ever since he got the cold and cough he could not shake. That must be three or four months by now.

The most difficult thing, he finds, is the letting go, the release of control. All his life, he has fallen on his knees at night, convinced he was giving himself over to his Maker, but now he realizes that was not entirely so. He was a landowner, after all, who, apart from his dependence on the elements, directed his own destiny. And he was a labourer, every tool and piece of machinery functioning smoothly because of his clear head and steady hands.

He wishes his hands were steady like that again. In his prime, he could pull apart and put things together as well as any man he knew. Even in retirement, he built things out of cast off pieces as if they were new materials. He stares down at his hands and wonders who will pick up the chair pieces in the alley and what that person will make with them. He hopes his chair will not be used for firewood.

No, letting go is not easy. What will he do when his body completely fails him? He can still make it to the bathroom the dozens of times a day he has to go, but he knows it will not be long before that changes. He can still get to the table, too. He dreads the time when he will require feeding, as did his stroke-stricken mother and gangrenous mother-in-law. He hates the thought of Arlene slipping her right hand under his chin to keep his head up. He imagines soup sliding down the corners of his mouth and wrenches his head to the side.

The family makes a big production of moving Arlene's chair into the corner his was in. Karla reminds him the new chair will arrive tomorrow. "Today is Sunday," she explains, "the stores aren't open." He knows that. His relatives would never leave their farms and drive the hour-and-a-half to visit any other day.

I am dying, he wants to shout. If I didn't need a new chair last week when I wasn't dying, why do I need one this week? He wants to shout other things, too. He wants to shout that his allotted time was insufficient. He had not built that cabinet his wife wanted. He had not talked to Karla and her brothers, Eric and Nathan, about the value of slowing down because life is too short. And he would not see his grandchildren, Laurel and Jennifer, grow from cavorting imps to vital young women.

He would also like to shout about his past: the father who died before he was born; the mother who moved him into various church rectories to support them by cooking and cleaning; and the priests whose doleful eyes bored through him each time he removed his white tunic after mass.

But, because he is known as a quiet man who never causes trouble, he sits down in Arlene's chair, its lumps all wrong, and reaches for his spittle can. The can has been moved. Arlene hustles over to get it for him before she brings out the coffee and carrot cake. The talk goes in and out of his head. He hears something about crops, crops too wet to take off in the fall, and remembers the time it snowed so early his wheat stayed out in the fields all winter. He sees himself descend the cellar stairs of the old farm house, to count the jars of preserved food and cold storage items: forty quarts each of carrots, peas, corn, tomatoes and beans; thirty quarts each of chicken, beef stew and meatballs; five sacks of potatoes; and a sawdust bin full of carrots and pungent turnips. Enough, perhaps, if no relative other than his wife and children look to him for assistance throughout the winter. They will have to give up store bought things, though, like peanut butter, tobacco, and coffee. Hating the thought of a whole winter without tobacco and coffee, he makes up his mind to buy a John Deere combine next summer.

"Remember those old threshing machines and crews," his nephew, Frank, says. His ears prick up. He pushes forward to rock the chair and becomes frustrated because this is Arlene's chair and it is stationary. He does remember the threshing crews, however. It was on account of their late arrival his wheat stayed out that year and he had been forced to work for the CNR to buy the combine. Of all the years he had feared losing crops to early snowfall, he only recalls it actually happening once. He is glad, though, it forced him to take action.

At times, he had acted too late. He quit smoking fifteen years ago, but it should have been thirty. He pictures himself then, roll-your-own cigarette hanging from his mouth while he herded cattle, bareback on Tom, or swung a sledgehammer to imbed railroad ties. It is not an ugly picture; he liked smoking and the manliness it represented. The ugly picture is the time he and his mother had been so destitute they could not afford his weekly can of Vogue tobacco and Chanticleer papers. He remembers how his mother managed to buy him tobacco one week and the tears it brought to his eyes. Tears well up now.

Such a gift! If only he had known then. But, given his observance of the younger generation, he realizes the unlikelihood of making early changes. Oh, to be wise as he is now and still possess the enthusiasm of youth. He shakes his head at that foolhardy young man who managed to talk the bank into lending him the money to buy the farm. He was only eighteen years old. He still has the photographs of himself and his mother, their first day out there, standing on a bare knoll in front of the old log house: he, in peaked cap and overalls; and she in a long black dress and laced boots.

Buying that quarter section of land was the best thing he ever did. He remembers the thrill of it. Watching each plant sprout into the spring air. Helping infant animals ease themselves out of the womb. Holding his hands under the wheat auger to catch the fruits of his labour.

And the thrill that coursed through his broad chest when he met Arlene at a family wedding has never been surpassed. He still thanks God for that chance pairing. And he thanks God for the children.

Ah, the children. He loved nothing better than to stand back and watch Eric and Nathan toboggan down the pasture hills on the apparatuses he bent and shaped out of scrap tin. Or to steer Karla around the skating rink he had poured by filling barrels of water and clucking at his horses to pull them home to the garden.

How he enjoyed the winter nights with them, playing cards under the light of a kerosene lamp, the aroma of Arlene's maple fudge emanating from the Mcleary Easy cook stove. Bids and laughter and sticky fingers filled the long, dark hours while coyotes on nearby hills howled and the animals in the barn huddled.

They had huddled, too. Arlene's hands constantly clacked a pair of knitting needles to keep the family in wool socks, scarves, mitts, and toques. And she carded more wool for blankets than he thought fair for one woman to do. The house, heated by an enormous coal furnace which invariably smouldered out through the night, would be so cold he had to rise early to stoke it. And, he had cut so many piles of firewood for the kitchen stove he had lost count of them over the years. Nature's work, which took years to grow, cut up and burnt within a matter of hours. So wasteful, he thinks, visualizing the chair pieces in the alley.

"Uncle George," his niece, Beryl, says, "do you remember how we used to guess the temperature by how thick the ice had formed overnight on the pail of drinking water?"

"Ah, yes," he says, "but, exactly where did Frank and Theo put the pieces?" No one answers, so he knows it did not come out in words. He smiles, liking the time frame they're talking about. It was so primitive, so virile.

He thinks of his virility. Recalls how he had liked cupping his hand between Arlene's legs after he made love to her. He would lie there like that all night, fingers flexing now and then, if she did not move. Now, he must rely on memory for an erection and ejaculation. It is fading. He only thinks of it on occasion. He wants to warn Eric and Nathan about this, but sex is not a topic he has ever felt comfortable discussing. He tried once. Concerned over Eric, who was far too young to spend so much time with a girl, he said: "Son, it might be a good idea for us to buy you some condoms. We don't want any accidents, do we?"

"You're crazy, Dad," was the answer he got. He had decided to mind his own business after that, even though he had to eventually arrange a snap wedding.

And, his daughter, Karla; what could he have said to her when he passed her bedroom door and saw her mopping up the bed with a towel?

"I spilled coffee all over the bed," she had said when she noticed him watching her.

Yes, Karla, he had thought. He supposed that was possible. But were there not two cups on the bed stand and had he not pulled out the hide-a-bed in the living room the night before for that young rooster to sleep on?

He reaches down to the handle to lift up the foot rest. The confounded thing is not where it is supposed to be. He wants to slam the side of this foreign object, but not being a demonstrative man, he tries again. He begins to cough. The cough comes from deep within him. He imagines the numerous spots on his lungs and coughs harder in hope of spitting the blasted things up.

Theo walks over to him and releases the chair handle. His feet and legs lift up too fast, but the sudden rush startles him enough to stop the coughing. He accepts coffee and cake from Theo's wife, Samantha, who is carrying the serving tray. He stirs and stirs and stirs the sugar into his coffee, as he has always done. He stops himself, thinking, what's the use? Nothing has taste anymore.

That's what he told Karla when she last took him out for lunch. She had ordered him an omelet and a thick slice of Spanish onion. "When I was a kid, it was your favourite," she had said, smiling out of those thin lips he had surely passed on to her. As he looked at her, he noticed the lips were not all he had passed on. She had his deep-set eyes, a little greener perhaps, and the thin hair, and the square jaw with just a hint of the jowls she would surely get. And she was quiet and determined. He had made a mental note to come back to her after he was gone, to see how she was doing; perhaps in one of her dreams. He would walk beside her for a while on a city street and ask her. He does not think of returning to Eric and Nathan. They are men, after all, and will get on fine.

Arlene must be awake when I come to her, he thinks. The raspberry patch stands out in his mind as the perfect location. He knows she will go there a lot to keep her hands busy. He visualizes her hands, the right one holding a white bowl, the left reaching toward the raspberries. He sees her long fingers curve around the luscious red fruit, arthritic knuckles protruding somewhat.

His own knuckles protrude. And his hands shake. He tries not to spill the coffee from the fancy china cup his wife thought nice to use for company. In the melee of things, she must have forgotten to provide a mug. He needs to go to the bathroom, so decides to get up and get himself a decent sized cup at the same time. The chair handle hampers him again. Up on his feet finally, he shuffles to the bathroom. He dreads the pain of passing water, is not sure which is worse, the force of the urge or the burn of urination. The doctors have ruled out removing part of his prostate gland because of the strain on heart and lungs.

"There's nothing to be done, but at least I'm at home," he mutters, as he fumbles with his zipper. He leans over, holding the wall with one hand. A small amount of urine dribbles into the bowl. He grimaces and leans harder on the wall. No more. He shakes his penis and tucks it back into his pants. His hands tremble as he does up the zipper. He washes his hands feeling agitated; the whole procedure will have to be repeated in less than half an hour.

Back in the main part of the house, he notices bits of the brown and white striped fabric from his old chair on the carpet. He slowly bends down and picks one up. He tucks it into the breast pocket of his shirt and returns to the chair. If there had been a piece of wood left, he would have picked that up, too.

"That chair wasn't very solid anymore, Uncle George," Frank says, keying in ever so slightly to his thoughts.

"Neither am I," he says. He wants to turn around and go to his room, but company is here and he must be polite, so he sits down again. He has forgotten about fetching a mug. He rocks back and forth a few times, then stops and fishes for the upholstery in his pocket. He lays it smooth on his knee, looks at it for a long time trying to remember the delivery men who brought him the chair. He cannot bring them to mind. It bothers him because he knows everyone in the area. Perhaps they moved. He wonders if that will happen after he dies, if people will remember a circumstance, but maybe forget he was in it. He hopes not. He picks up the fabric and rubs it between his fingers. It feels rough. He thinks of the plush fabric his wife described as being on the new navy-blue chair and wonders if he will even notice it, given that the green work pants and long-sleeved shirt he always wears leaves little skin exposed.

The talk centres on going home now, fields to plough the next day, and machinery to be fixed. He does not know if he will see them again. They kiss him goodbye and talk about the wonders of modern medicine. He sees the tears in their eyes and hears the breaks in their voices. Perhaps they will remember him. Dry-eyed, he kisses each one back and nods his head to their reassurances.

As the door closes on them, he tries to forgive them for tearing his chair apart and hauling it out so irreverently. This is not a time to hold grudges. He has never done it before, not even against the priests. Had he done so, he would not have the faith he needs to get through this. "God, please help me forgive one more time," he says. It comes out louder than he wanted it to, but his wife and daughter are washing the dishes and do not hear him. "And give me courage to face this," he adds.

He rubs the piece of striped upholstery between his fingers thinking about those who have preceded him; his mother, sister, aunts, uncles, and friends. A pair of brown eyes appear before him. To his dismay, they are not human. They belong to his spirited horse, Tom. Tom, who balked at wearing a bridle or being hitched to wagon or sleigh. Tom, who pawed the ground in anticipation of the gallop. Tom, who did not jump high enough one day and impaled himself on a fence post. He remembers having to run at a gallop himself for his .22 calibre gun. And trying to avoid looking into Tom's eyes before he shot him.

The eyes hold him now, in a steady gaze. They are young and carefree. He blinks, then closes his eyes and imagines lighting on Tom's back. It is dusk and they lope through the thickening darkness, long and hard. They reach a gate. He pulls back on the reins to stop Tom so he can dismount and open it, but Tom continues on and jumps the gate. The ascent is like taking wing and feels freer than he has ever experienced. When they land, it is dawn. The sun bursts yellow and the dew on the wild grass glistens. The horse stops and remains still despite the clack of tongue and flail of reins.

Opening his eyes, he sees that the rein he is flailing is just the scrap of upholstery. He bites his tongue and steadies his hands somewhat, then holds the fabric up to the waning light. As he turns it about to examine all the colours and feel the weave, he wills his thumb and index finger to separate and release the fabric. It drifts in a sudden breeze coming through the open window and settles on a sun-patch in the middle of the living room floor.

Undertow: Short Fiction